I0677585

THE MAN IN THE PINES

A Novel
by David
Nash

The Man in the Pines
Copyrighted © 2020 David Nash
ISBN 978-1-64538-129-7
First Edition

The Man in the Pines
by David Nash

All Rights Reserved. Written permission must be secured from the publisher to use
or reproduce any part of this book, except for brief quotations in critical reviews or
articles.

For information, please contact:

www.ten16press.com
Waukesha, WI

Edited by Lauren Blue
Cover design by Kaeley Dunteman

This book is a work of fiction. Names, characters, places, and incidents are the
product of the author's imagination or are used fictitiously. Characters in this
book have no relation to anyone bearing the same name and are not based on
anyone known or unknown to the author. Any resemblance to actual businesses or
companies, events, locales, or persons, living or dead, is coincidental.

For my family, friends,
and everything worth fighting for.

Minnesota Summer, 1983

Dust dances in the morning light
There's a chickadee outside my door
Little feathers only matter
When the ruler's keeping score

The dusty pine boards creaked under his feet as he shuffled from one end of the cabin to the other. He stopped and pressed his thick hands on the edge of the sink basin. The white soapstone was cold to the touch. He let out a coarse sigh, feeling the heat exchange between his leathery, arthritic hands and the cool sink.

In his old age, shrunken and thinning, his hunched shoulders covered by a shirt of deep crimson plaid told the story of a body once strong and fierce. His frame was, even now, startlingly large compared to most elderly men. His shoulders could fill a doorframe, and his hands were like the paws of a weathered grizzly from years and years of labor. He took a deep breath in through his nose and lifted his gaze out the window into the forest where adolescent pines surrounded the cabin. The scraggly, grayish jack pines were already dwarfed by the stately Norways. He let out a quiet laugh, noticing how the glass in the window seemed to have warped with time.

"You too?" he said.

The distorted glass gave the impression that he was looking through a waterfall, and he tilted his head slightly for a view of the path down to the lake, its edges softened by the encroaching tree branches. Between the leaves, small wisps of light burst into a kaleidoscope of haloes as the sun climbed above the trees. For all he knew, it was just as likely his clouding cataracts playing out this scene as it was the glass. Didn't really matter either way.

He pushed off the sink and turned to the door. The old man let out a groan in response to the aching pains swarming his knees as if the joints were filled with enraged hornets. He didn't know if it was the floor or his bones that were creaking and cracking as he reached for the oiled wooden handle of the double-bit ax that leaned on the doorframe. The blades were sharp but had been whittled down to stubs by decades of use.

The front of the cabin had a small covered porch sprinkled with dried, burnt-orange pine needles and patches of moss and lichen. A few rusted saw blades, the tallest of which pushed eight feet in length, had been leaned against the railing long ago and were now sagging under their own weight. By the door sat a solitary wooden chair with a dirty cloth hanging off the back. An assortment of weather-worn canteens and a large harness hung from square nails jutting out of the posts holding up the roof. The leather straps of the harness were cracked and stiff from the elements. The old man ducked through the doorway and let the door clap shut behind him. There, he paused to look at the harness and, closing his eyes, pictured the last time he had slid it over his friend's ears and cold, pale nose. It had been hanging untouched for so long now that he supposed if he lifted it off the nail, it would shatter into a thousand pieces.

The man turned and reached for the muddy sheet dangling on the chair, then swung it over his shoulder, feeling a few remaining saplings resting in the damp folds of the fabric against his side. He'd need to gather more before the walk to the edge of the forest.

"Are you comin' today, or are you just gonna sit there?"

He hadn't seen the rabbit, but he knew it was there. It was always there each morning at the base of the lush elderberry bush on the east side of the cabin. He looked to his right, and there lay the grayish, sandy-brown rabbit with the faint, rusty patch of fur behind its neck. It sat, eyeing the old man, twitching its nose and sending its whiskers into a vibratory frenzy. He turned away from the animal and slowly made his way around the porch, walking away from the path to the lake.

The morning air was refreshing, but still. As long as a storm didn't roll in, the day had the potential to be a good one. He figured that if he could find enough saplings this morning, he could finish the last acre of the forest before sundown.

After two hours of walking circles further and further from the cabin, every so often kneeling and gently digging with the corner of his chipped ax to uproot small, bright green, soft pines, his makeshift satchel was sagging full with the harvest. *That should be plenty*, he thought, looking at the dense bunch of emerald green needles poking out beneath his arm.

The sun was at its peak by the time he made his way to the clearing. Where there once stood a massive aspen grove on the mostly level ground now was a wide swath of open field. Piles of decaying aspen logs fenced the space, which stretched just to the end of his view as if following the curvature of the Earth. At first glance, one could mistake it for a wide bramble of shrubbery and blueberry bushes, but looking closer, varying sizes of pale-green pine saplings rooted themselves in an orderly fashion, covering nearly the entire expanse. Gazing over the young grove, the old man stood up a little taller at the sight of his work. *It's a start*, he thought. *A new beginning. The place where my old pines can grow again.* His mind drifted to the miles and miles of similar groves he'd planted in these northern forests over many, many years. *How many years has it been? Twenty? Thirty? Who knows?*

As he pondered the thousands of trees planted, a darting shape in his periphery caught his attention.

"It's about time you showed up. I'm just about to plant the last of 'em," the man said.

The rabbit stared at him coolly as if to say, "Yes, it's about time."

The man scoffed at the sad reality that this rabbit was his closest companion and, quite literally, the only thing he'd spoken to in years. He couldn't quite figure out why the animal continued to show up or even how it was possible that it had lived so long, but the answers to these details didn't seem worth exploring for someone who had lived a life filled with events that defied reality. His strength left his body years ago. The details had long since faded, and he just didn't have the energy to try and recall them anymore.

He turned away from the hare. "I don't know why you insist on watching me. The least you could do is lend a hand." At this, the rabbit made a quick shift in its weight and sped off in the opposite direction. "Thought so," the man said to himself before returning to the grove.

He made his way to the far corner of the clearing. The ground was bumpy in places littered with large, exposed slabs of granite, but remained essentially flat. Some areas looked freshly tilled, while the stubble of recently cut aspens spread elsewhere. Patches of knee-high weeds and grasses filled in gaps between rotting tree stumps, the last remnants of the tall giant pines that once ruled this land. He paced the empty corner of the grove, walking in long, straight lines. Following each expansive stride, he bent down and drove two fingers deep into the ground, which was quickly followed by a sudden shove that left a freshly transplanted white pine to ponder its newfound home. He then clawed a wide circle around the sapling to clear away any competitors for the soil.

After a few hours of planting, the sun decided that this was enough work for the day. The mid-afternoon black flies had retired, and the first waves of mosquito clouds were beginning their shift. The old man slowly stood up and arched his back to stretch, looking out at the vast field of young pines. In spite of everything, he couldn't help but notice the spark of pride, and even something close to happiness, fluttering deep in his chest, and he wondered how long it had been since he had felt such things.

The bed in the warped wooden cabin was calling his name. Tonight, he would sleep well. After one last look over the field that he had spent the previous few months planting, he swung his ax over his shoulder and began the long trudge home. Sleep. He needed sleep.

———

"Paul...Paul..." The girl wore a soft vanilla blouse with long sleeves that tapered at her wrists. Her dress was a deep chestnut shade of brown that bloomed as it dropped to her feet. A soft smile favoring one side of her mouth greeted him as he met her gaze. "Paul..." She spoke his name again, though her lips didn't move. He wanted to reach out to her. Oh, how he wanted to grab her tightly and hold her in his arms, but his body didn't seem to be in this dream. He was a shapeless visitor. Or was she visiting him?

Again, he heard her voice. "Paul..." He tried to call out to her. Tried to yell her name. But she kept on smiling until her lips parted and she mouthed, "Help." He couldn't tell if this was a plea or an instruction. He tried to reach out to her, but she closed her eyes and, turning, began walking away. He shouted. He screamed until his throat burned. The burning spread throughout his body, and soon flames rose around him. She was somewhere in the fire. Again he tried to call for her and tried to reach out, but tongues of flame leapt about his hands, peeling the skin as they wrapped tightly around him like a thousand terrible snakes.

Bolting upright from the nightmare, he knew he'd been thrashing. The sheets were twisted around his torso just like the flames in his dream. Shards of wood covered his body, and the cold night air leaked into the cabin, giving him a chill. It was as if a meteor had crashed into the wall beside him. Slivers of moonlight sliced through the logs to his left like daggers, and his elbow ached from the blow that caused the destruction during his nightmare.

The old man tried to shut his eyes and find her again, but it was no use. She was gone. Her soft cheekbones and dark eyes, just as he had known them, had walked away into the burning emptiness of sleep. He was alone. *As it began, so it ends,* he thought. *I came into this world alone. Might as well leave it that way.*

As he lay back down in the cloudless night of the northern woods of Minnesota, his thoughts drifted to another storm. A storm long ago that brought him into the arms of two strangers who would come to love him for the child he was and the giant he would become.

Winter Storm, 1870

Lonely.
I am lonely.
I am with him,
But I am alone.
Give me
A child
So that I may
Feel whole.

Andrew Cunningham and his wife, Samantha, had been doing their best to survive the winter, but the cold weather was finally getting to them. The great state of Maine had served them a run of storms that had hammered the coast with feet of snow and chilled them to the bone. It was well regarded that this might be one of the worst winters in history. To make matters worse, two months earlier, Samantha had suffered her third miscarriage. She was beginning to think that either her body couldn't handle pregnancy after the fifth month or God didn't intend for her to have children after all.

She had held each of her children in her hands as their fragile bodies slowly lost the warmth she had given them. To Samantha, they were her children fully formed and realized, but now lost. Andrew struggled with the losses in his own way, but she knew it wasn't the same for him. He didn't love them the way she did. She could feel him starting to think about trying again but wondered whether her heart could withstand another loss.

The shutters on their single-room farmhouse rattled in the wind. Andrew tossed another log on the fire, sending up a flurry of sparks from the glowing coals.

"Heaven, help us! The roof will cave in if this storm doesn't let up soon!" Andrew eyed the rafters uneasily. He liked to think he was as good a carpenter as any, but he couldn't help but question his craftsmanship during a storm like this.

"That, or we'll be buried in the drifts of snow that are piling up." Samantha smiled back at him, thankful to be taken out of her darker ruminations.

Andrew was pacing now. "That wind is wailin'! I could swear it sounds like a screamin' child."

Samantha had thought so too, but had pushed it from her mind. Her tendency for tears was high enough without the hallucinations of a crying baby. *A crying child is better than no child*, she thought.

Another howling wind slammed the side of the house, rattling the boards like the ribcage of a skeleton, sending shockwaves across Andrew and Samantha's skin. With every gust, Samantha thought the crying was getting louder and sounding more childlike, less like the gale of a great blizzard. "You're hearing this, aren't you?" she shot at Andrew.

"Of course I hear it! This storm is going to be the end of us, I'm telling you. The house is even cryin' now." But even as he said it, he could tell that something in the wind had changed.

They looked at each other, then both nervously turned toward the rattling door. Flurries of snow were finding their way through the edges of the frame along with the whimpering cries that had grown louder and more frantic with each passing breath. In Andrew's moment of hesitation, Samantha rushed to the door and flung it open. A cyclone of snowflakes and whistling wind greeted her, but there at her feet lay a child, swaddled and squirming and evidently furious, red-faced from either the cold or the constant screaming.

"Andrew," Samantha called.

"Shut the door, Sam! What in heaven's name are you doing?" Having already forgotten about the strange screaming, he had settled next to the small fire and was coaxing it with an iron rod.

"It's a baby..." she said in a stunned voice as a powdery layer of snow accumulated on her dress.

"What's a baby?" Andrew asked, still focusing his energy on thawing his backside.

"At the door. The crying. It's a baby." Samantha reached down and lifted the child into her arms. Absentmindedly, she shut the door with her shoulder, never stopping to look anywhere else but the child's small, rosy face. "You're a heavy little thing, aren't you?" She brushed the clusters of frozen tears from the baby's eyelashes, then cooed. The baby opened his eyes wide and stopped crying immediately. It was in that mere moment that Samantha felt complete for the first time. A magnetic force was pulling her to this infant and filling a void that had haunted her for years. Her branches had finally found their leaves.

Andrew tentatively made his way to Samantha's side. His eyebrows raised with uncertainty as he watched his wife cradle the baby. He thought she looked like a painting, made to hold the infant forever. Still, Andrew wasn't sure what to think about this unexplained arrival. "Samantha...don't you think maybe we should just leave that child be?"

Samantha looked down into the infant eyes that grew drowsier by the second, eyes like dark stones from a riverbed, and calmly said, "No. We won't leave him be. Now, where did you come from, my sweet little thing?"

And with that, the child yawned an adult-sized yawn and promptly fell asleep.

―――

The Cunninghams had always been a somewhat nomadic people. Andrew was a first-generation American, his parents having come from Scotland during their early childhoods. He and Samantha grew up together in Massachusetts on nearby homesteads and were married before they turned sixteen. Both had dreamed of exploring the wild country of the Americas and yearned for land they could farm and use to raise a family. When the children didn't come, the possibility of farming moved further and further from practicality. A successful farm relied on a consistent collection of hardworking hands, and a large family provided that. Without sons and daughters at his side, Andrew was left to do most of the harder labor himself. To be sure, Samantha picked up more than her share of the physical work. She had a knack for unleashing strength that often surprised Andrew. He assumed that part of it was the frustration of being childless. He insisted on being the one to chop the firewood, but Samantha was relentless and demanded he accept her help. She swung an ax smoothly and swiftly, proving that it wasn't strength but a precise blow that split a log with ease.

In 1870, Samantha and Andrew opened the door on a blizzard and closed it on their childless lives. They couldn't explain how their son, whom they named Paul, arrived. As far as they knew, there wasn't another family for at least ten miles. The idea that someone had been outside in a storm of that severity was sheer madness. Strange that they would come that close to shelter and not linger to partake in the warmth of the fire but simply leave this treasure and move on. Stranger still, they couldn't explain how Samantha was nursing Paul within the first day. Fearful that the question alone would cut off her supply, she didn't dare ask how or why her body began tingling that stormy night he arrived and why her milk came the next morning. So while Andrew never moved past an underlying suspiciousness of how conveniently this baby filled an emptiness for his wife, Samantha accepted her role as mother wholeheartedly and without hesitation. She felt that Paul was intended for her and her alone. In turn, she gave him everything.

———

Paul was a precocious child, walking at six months and talking in short sentences by one year. More importantly, he was deftly swinging a hatchet at two years old. With pant legs that swayed above his ankles and shirtsleeves that were quickly outgrown, he would walk with his wide gait, toddler belly protruding, and pick up a small quarter-split log with both hands. From the doorway of their home, Samantha would watch as Paul balanced the log straight up, picked up his hatchet, and with one full-body swing, cut the wood in two, giggling all the while. His hair grew black and thick with grapevine curls, and his eyes were usually the color of a stormy, bottomless lake, but they tended to shift with the weather and his mood. One day they might be black as night, and another they would be gray as morning fog. A day later, his eyes would radiate with violets and blues.

The Cunninghams traveled around the outskirts of Bangor for several years while Paul was young. His father picked up small jobs here and there, eventually settling on selling elixirs he created in the back of their wagon. Every new village on the horizon was an opportunity to hang his stenciled sign exclaiming the wonders of his cure-all potion, which was mostly various forms of dilute opium. All the while, Samantha nurtured Paul, and he grew like a weed. No shirtsleeves or pant legs were too long.

The uncertainty and restlessness of one parent impressed upon Paul just as much as the unflappable love of the other. By the time he was eight, he knew he wanted an honest way of living. The unreliability of a "magic" elixir and the lack of control of not only its effects but also the patron's response was something he grew to hate. He craved hard labor, even from a young age. Chopping firewood at each stop along their travels was a tangible task. There was no mystery to the way the wood split and turned into either a home or fuel. Whenever they came to a logging town, he would watch the crews sitting high atop piles of logs loaded for transport to the mills. The teamster would give a whoop, and the oxen would dig their hooves into the mud, driving the haul to its destination. What a sight, those champions of the ax, conquerors of the forest. He dreamed of nothing but becoming one of them.

Still, Paul noticed that many of those men sat listlessly with an emptiness in their eyes. Their heads swayed as they bobbed back and forth on top of their kills. They didn't have the passion and pride that he learned from his mother. She was a woman of strength. Samantha executed every task with honesty and a clear destination. Neither sewn thread nor shoed horse was half-hearted. She was the epitome of mindfulness and determination. When it was his turn to ride the pines, ax in hand, swinging his way through the trees, he would carry all of his mother's lessons and, as a result, be a logger second to none.

At ten years old, the path to Paul's lumberjack daydreams began to take shape. It was a late summer afternoon. Paul and a few town children were rolling hoops past one of the local lumber mills when he overhead a group of young men bragging about their upcoming adventures in the logging camps. Six of them were standing in a circle, jockeying back and forth.

"I'll be spending five months this winter up near the border," a tall, blond-haired boy with patchy facial hair proudly announced to his companions.

"I bet you don't make it past January, Henry," the shortest young man shot back, laughing with the others who were nudging elbows in agreement.

"At least I'll be up there! I've been waiting four years now, and my pa finally agreed. Said I was old enough to support the family, he did." The blond boy was blushing but standing his ground.

Jabs between the group slowed down as jealousy and interest grew at the thought of an adventure in the big woods. Paul stood, riveted by the conversation. It was the first time he'd heard someone spell out a plan to work in the woods.

"Hey, kid, what're you looking at?" The short fellow had noticed Paul as he stared, mouth agape, at the group.

Paul was startled back from the daydream that these boys unwittingly incited, one where he pictured himself standing in a similar circle telling his friends about his upcoming winter expedition to seek out the pines. "Oh, sorry. Nothin'," Paul mumbled, then turned his back on the jeering laughs tossed in his direction. One day soon, that would be him leaving to join the logging teams of Maine.

While Paul knew his future path at an abnormally young age, Samantha knew it even earlier. She knew he was destined for the tall trees. She could see it in the way he stared at them as they drove their wagon through the countryside and by the way he smiled when he picked up his father's ax, even when he wasn't supposed to lay a hand on it. And while Andrew struggled to find common ground and create a bond with Paul, he seemed to show his support in the form of passive assent to the idea that his son would leave the family business and forge his own unique path. Every time Paul finished his chores and asked to sharpen the ax or borrow it to practice his swing, Andrew let him go. After all, if there was one thing that he had in common with his son, it was that he, too, once desired to leave and find adventure on his own. Paul would have to discover for himself if the punchline of life's cruel joke was failure or glory, and Andrew knew from experience which was more likely.

Just as much as Paul was comforted by his mother, he was driven by his father's high emotional walls. For when a boy is loved so deeply by his mother, how can he not try to win his father's affection? When Andrew Cunningham made the decision, whether conscious or not, to guard his heart against this boy, it was as if a seed had been planted in Paul, a seed that would grow into a towering pine of motivation. From an early age, Paul was already looking for ways to show his father that he was deserving of his love, that he was someone that would make his father proud, a man to admire.

Departure, August 1884

What was once so small
And couldn't live without you,
Every day has taken one step closer
To leaving you completely.
It is sobbing at home alone.
It is a geyser of pride.
It is bitter for you.
It is sweet for them.

"Pa! Pa!" Paul Cunningham bounded down the dusty lane flanked by knee-high prairie grass. He leapt over large puddles as he headed outside of town to find his father. He found Andrew lying on his back, peering at the broken axle of their horseless wagon, which rattled from Paul's approaching footsteps. "Pa, did you see the posting in town at the mill? Everyone's talkin' about it."

Andrew Cunningham wiggled his way out from beneath the wagon and turned over onto his knees. After rocking back onto his feet, he achingly rose and dusted off his hands. He looked up at his son, who stood nearly a foot taller than his own six-foot frame. "I did," was all he said, and he turned to walk up to the cabin.

"You did? When? Never mind. Pa, they're hiring!" Paul stopped and watched his dad's back, looking for an indication, an answer to the unasked question.

Andrew stood still for a long moment, head hung low as he pretended to focus on his boots. The brown leather looked black from the years of hard work. He dragged the heel of his left boot across the inside of the right to scrape a clump of dried mud free from the leather. "Does your mother know?"

"No, not yet I expect." When Paul first saw that the lumber mill was recruiting more men to head north, he, of course, first thought of his mother. He knew she wouldn't want him to go. She wanted him to wait at least another year until he was fifteen, and Paul knew how much his parents relied on his help with the day-to-day work. He told her he would send money each month, what little there may be, but Samantha's foot was rooted firmly in the ground, and she was as stubborn as their ox. That was why Paul came to his father first, hoping his support would be helpful in swaying the strong will of his mother.

"So, you think you're ready to go off and work then?" Andrew glanced up at his son.

"I do. I mean, I *am* ready. I'm near twice the size of the other boys my age and can swing an ax just as well as any grown man." He was showing his youth with this protest, and he knew it, so he paused and took a deep breath, trying to slow down. "I'm ready, Pa. I can do more for this family logging and sending the money home than I can by staying here, touring around selling elixirs and helping Ma fix the barn. I know we don't have much money."

Andrew raised his eyebrows. "You do, do you? And you think you running off chopping down trees will be the thing that saves this family?" He shook his head in frustration and pointed north, his voice rising. "It's hard out there, Paul. Those are rough men. They don't mess around when it's working time. They're bound to give you a hard time as well. They'll try and break you. Get you to come home cryin'. I don't care how big you are, they will try their best to prove you're just a child." He stopped to let his words sink in, and his mind drifted to the baby that blew into their lives nearly fifteen years ago. As the memories surfaced, his voice softened. "Do you think you can handle that?"

"I do," Paul said, lifting his shoulders and standing a shade taller, which happened to be a fraction shorter than the nearest young chestnut tree.

This subtle act of posturing always startled Andrew and reminded him just how big his little child really was. *Oh, my boy, everyone shrinks in your shadow*, he thought.

"Let's talk to your mother tonight." Andrew kneeled back down to the dirt and the wagon axle, hoping his son knew how much he cared for him but unsure how to show it. He looked back up to Paul. "I was gonna get some men to help lift this wagon onto a block if you'd like to give us a hand."

"Sure, Pa, but we can take care of it. I can lift it on my own."

"Don't be a fool. You'll hurt yourself. It won't take long to find a few hands."

"It'll be fine. Honest."

Andrew looked at Paul through the corner of his narrowing eyes.

Paul stood next to the wagon, which came up past his waist and stretched nearly six feet wide. A few large stones rested on the floorboards from clearing the neighbor's field the week before.

"At least get those stones out of there first, Paul."

"It's alright. I've got it." Paul bent his knees, and with a deep exhale and both hands gripped firmly on the underside of the wagon, he lifted it about a foot off the ground.

Andrew Cunningham stared up at him, mesmerized at the herculean strength of his boy, this young man.

"I may be making it look light, Pa, but be assured it ain't," Paul said through gritted teeth.

"Right," Andrew replied, and he got back to work.

———

Samantha had feared this day for years. She thought she'd have a few more seasons with her son, but parents never see their children as grown no matter the inches nor the years. Bearded or not, he would always be her little boy, rescued from a cold winter storm and nursed by her love. But just as much as she wanted to hold on tightly, he wanted to seize his independence and stand on his own, as all children eventually do.

"Water's in the basin. Wash up, boys, before the stew gets cold."

She knew what was coming before they spoke. The air stiffened as they walked into the room dimly lit by two kerosene lanterns. The two men found their seats at the table, and Samantha waited for them to begin the conversation. Patience was one of her most potent weapons.

After several minutes of heads bowed over soup bowls and slurping sounds from all, Paul couldn't stand it any longer.

"Mama?" It was as much a plea as a question.

She turned to her boy, met his eyes, and waited for him to continue.

"The mill is asking for more help up north. I...I'd like to go. Folks say the woods in Michigan and Wisconsin are filled with even more timber to harvest, but I'll stay closer," he was quick to add.

Samantha knew this was a lie. She knew it wouldn't be long before he'd move westward, but she let him continue.

"I can send money home each month to help you and Pa, and I'll come back and visit all the time."

This she believed, but both the money and visits home would be less than he realized. "You've talked to your father about this, I suppose?"

She glanced in Andrew's direction, but he was intensely inspecting a chip in the edge of his empty bowl.

"I have. Just before supper."

"And what do you think, Andrew?"

Looking to his son's pleading face, he took a deep breath. "I think he'll do fine. You're a strong boy, and you know it. Just need to keep your head when around all those shanty men out there. Can't let anyone take advantage of you, you hear me?"

Samantha had anticipated this response from her husband, but she wasn't going to give up easily. "So that's it? We're gonna let our little boy go off and live with heaven knows what kind of men before he's fully grown?"

"He's not a little boy, Sam. He's at least as big as the other men, and you know well as I do that we could use the money." Andrew looked into his wife's eyes. She stared back at him, steady as stone, unwilling to yield. "And you don't have to worry about him suffering over the winter. I always hear the men talking about how well they take care of the jacks up north. Warm beds, plenty of food, and even music from time to time."

Samantha let this soak in before turning to her son. She knew he'd be going. She wasn't happy about it, but it did no good torturing him any longer.

"Paul, is this what you want? It's a hard life, and you could get hurt." Unlike Andrew, Samantha locked her eyes on her son's when she spoke to him.

"It is," he said in a tone he hoped was respectful and solemn, but it took all of his willpower to hold back his excitement as he felt the tide swaying in his direction.

"What matters most is who you are out there." His mother spoke softly but looked at him with an intensity that told him to pay close attention to her words. "You are going to be a leader. I've always known that. People are going to look up to you and say, 'There goes Paul Cunningham. I want to be just like him.' So, you're going to need to make sure you walk a path that leaves footprints you can be proud of. Those footprints can last a long time, and they can shape how others walk. And I want you to ask for help from time to time too. I know you like doing things on your own, but everyone needs help sometimes. Do you understand?"

"Mm-hmm...so, you'll let me go? And you'll be okay without me?" Even though this had been part of his argument, Paul craved the reassurance.

"We will let you go." *As if we'd really be able to keep him*, Samantha thought. "It seems your time has finally come. And yes, Paul, we'll be fine." She added the last part with an encouraging smile. Her son needed that little lie, otherwise he might never go. The last thing she wanted to do was to plant a seed of guilt in the boy's heart. To prevent that, she did her best to hide the bittersweet sadness clawing at her chest.

——

As August waned and the summer days began to shorten, Paul anxiously awaited joining the next group of shanty men heading up north into the remaining forests of Maine. The fact that there were fewer areas left to log in these woods gnawed at his excitement slightly, but word at the mill kept circling around the bountiful pineries of Michigan and Wisconsin and even some in Minnesota. As far as Paul was concerned, he'd cut his way across the land for the rest of his days.

It was the responsibility of each lumberjack to provide his own clothes and basic supplies, including an ax. It could take two months' wages before you'd have enough for an ax worth swinging. Paul knew his parents needed their ax and didn't dare ask for money to buy one before his departure, so his plan was to buy his logging equipment on credit at camp just like the rest of the jacks.

Paul was wading deeply through his thoughts as he cleaned out the barn that served as a shelter for their ox. The sour stench of manure mixed with the scent of dried hay and urine practically coated his tongue. He hated this chore most of all.

"Paul, you in there?" The voice of his father floated in through the broad wooden doors of the barn.

"Be right there, Pa." Paul moved toward the door as it swung open. His father walked in carrying a long object covered by a piece of tan canvas. Andrew wore the signs of a hard-lived life, knuckles littered with scars and deep worry lines carved into his forehead, but the middle-aged man was still muscular and sturdy. Andrew stopped for a moment to regain his grip on the object. It didn't go unnoticed by Paul that his father was taxed by the large parcel.

"I wanted to give you something before you go," he said, looking at the object in his hands. "You're a big lad. A regular ax won't do for you, especially since I have a feeling you're not done growing yet. Those camp cooks will feed you so well that you'll outgrow your clothes by springtime."

Paul nodded but didn't speak. Over the past few years, he had realized that he didn't really need to eat that much. He never got too hungry and only ate so his mother wouldn't get worried. One time, he went nearly a week without food just to see what would happen. Besides a little grumbling on the seventh day, he didn't lose an ounce of energy. Following the experiment, he went back to eating normally but added his diet to the growing list of things that made him a little different.

Andrew went on, "Anyway, I had this made up for you." He slid off the tarp and hoisted the ax into Paul's hands. Paul felt the sturdy weight of the wooden handle and looked toward the heavier end where he found a polished double-bit blade nearly the size of a snapping turtle. In the darkness of the barn, his reflection in the metal was ghost-like. He could just make out the face of a young man ready for adventure but unclear of his destination.

"Pa," was all he could muster. The ax was heavy, weighing almost as much as the gesture. Paul spread his hands across the extraordinary length of the handle, holding the bit in front of him. He lifted the ax with ease above his right shoulder and brought it down smoothly, digging into the imaginary tree trunk. Andrew watched with pride. When he'd raised the ax, it had felt like the tool was swinging him, but Paul made it look effortless.

Clearing his throat and avoiding his son's gaze, Andrew gave an awkward pat on Paul's shoulder. Paul began to speak, but Andrew interjected.

"Don't say anything. You deserve it, and anyway, this bigger ax should let you bring down more trees and hopefully send more money home, so the ax is really for me and your mother...in a way." He shrugged and gave Paul a grin, then turned to walk out of the barn. When he reached the door, he slowed for a moment, yelling over his shoulder, "Be sure to finish your chores before you go. Your mother will have my head if I let you go with that barn as messy as it is."

When he was alone, Paul inspected every inch of the ax. He ran his hands along the smooth handle and tested the blemish-free blade by scraping the back of his thumbnail across the edge. The white shavings piled up like snow sliding down a hillside. He gripped the ax and gave it a practice swing before reluctantly setting it aside to clean the rest of the barn before he lost the sunlight completely. He barely noticed the musty smell of the hay as his mind drifted to an image of himself swinging his ax through endless groves of towering trees. Today he finished his chores, but tomorrow he would begin the journey of a lifetime.

———

Before the sun rose the next morning, Andrew got dressed. Samantha woke to the sounds of her husband putting on his boots at the foot of their bed, and he told her that there was some business in town to tend to and asked her to tell Paul goodbye. She nodded as she put her arms around him, giving him a hug that lasted a little longer than usual. Then he left.

"It's just going to be us this morning," Samantha said to Paul as the two left the house for the train. "Your father had some things to take care of but told me to tell you goodbye for him."

A small wave of disappointment washed across Paul's eyes. "Oh. Alright," he said.

"I'll tell him you said goodbye as well, okay?"

"Sure. Thanks."

The rest of their walk was quiet until they walked into the railway station where men were busy loading crates and equipment. The workmen hollered back and forth, and the train hissed sporadically as if protesting the weight of the cargo it was sentenced to haul. Paul's ax was braced against his shoulder, and a small satchel hung below the double bit. The bag was filled with an extra shirt, a hat, some socks, stationery, and an old photograph of him which his mother insisted he keep. Paul remembered when the wagon had come through town with the camera a couple years earlier. He had been so excited he could barely sit still for the photographer. As far as he knew, he was the only boy who had gotten his picture taken, and for a long time, that had filled him with pride. Now it seemed a little silly. He took the photograph anyway.

The depot was as busy as Paul had seen it. There were men taking inventory of luggage and crates of cargo. A few greasy engineers were performing one last inspection of the engine. Nearby stood a cluster of seasoned lumberjacks. They passed around one last cigarette before departure and laughed at a dirty joke. About a dozen boys in their early teens were getting ready to leave their families for the first time. Their pink, unshaven faces traded nervous glances between their parents and the weathered men loading the trains. Paul recognized a few of the boys, and they exchanged nods. If there was anything Paul knew about logging, it was that pretty much anyone could become a jack if they could handle the work and avoid losing a limb. He eyed the rest of the crowds warily while his imagination conjured up stories of the people around him.

Paul glanced at a lanky, olive-skinned man with a clean, starched shirt and pants. With clothes that well pressed, this man was surely a gambler looking to escape debt collectors who had been cheated out of their money. The shifty, rat-faced gentleman to his left was undoubtedly trying to evade the law by the way his eyes darted back and forth. Paul imagined himself bursting through the crowd on horseback and running down the criminals. He would pick up both of the men by the backs of their shirts, one in each hand, like picking up kittens, and toss them at the feet of the town sheriff.

As Paul heard the scattered groups of immigrants speak in mysterious languages, he couldn't help but wonder if they were all talking about him, the freakishly tall greenhorn who'd be joining the crew. Just as his imagination and nerves were threatening to get the best of him, he spotted one of the storage cars being loaded with saws, axes, and cant hooks and remembered why he was standing in the train station with his mother at his side. Boarding this train might feel like jumping into a lake where you can't see the bottom, but to Paul, the excitement of becoming a real lumberjack won over all apprehension.

Still, just as any parent can, Samantha sensed the anxiety in her son as they approached the fray. "You'll be fine. Just keep your head down like your father said and stick to your work."

Paul kept his gaze on the men boarding the train. "I was hoping Pa could be here."

"I know. Me too. He wanted to, he really did."

Paul nodded but didn't speak. Even though his face hadn't changed, Samantha could see his sorrow turn to dismay.

That's just fine, Paul thought bitterly. *I don't need your help seein' me off anyway.*

Lingering glances that bordered on stares were starting to make their way towards him, as they usually did. In spite of his six-and-a-half foot, broad-shouldered frame, his face was still that of a young boy, dark hair shining as it curled out from behind his ears. Paul didn't give the staring more than a passing thought as the final calls came for the passengers to load the train.

Suddenly, his feet were rooted to the ground next to his mother. Leaving home, now that the moment was here, was not as easy and exciting as he thought it would be. Still, the only thing worse than leaving home was leaving as a whimpering mess. That would make him the laughingstock of the jacks. "There goes Paul Cunningham," they'd say, "the biggest baby in the land!" An image of crowds of people laughing and pointing in his direction flashed before his eyes.

With another deep breath, he adjusted the large ax over his shoulder and turned to say goodbye. "Thank you, Ma, for lettin' me go. Take care of Pa, will you? Tell him goodbye."

Samantha smiled. She didn't know what Paul's future held, but she always dreamed of him standing taller than trees and smiling broadly. She knew he would be fine. "Of course I will. Write when you can. We'll see you in the fall." *If we're lucky*, she thought. She had a feeling that once he got those big feet moving, he'd be gone for good.

With all the strength she could muster, she squeezed his hand one last time and turned to walk away so he wouldn't have to be seen hugging his tearful mother. The last thing she saw when she looked back was the crowd parting, staring up at her son. Every face was wearing the expression of awe that she felt in her heart daily.

———

The logging camps in Maine were in full swing when Paul went to work that first autumn. His skin tingled with excitement as he walked into camp with the other recruits. All around him, men shuffled back and forth, weaving in and out of one another with equal parts chaos and fluid coordination. Paul stood, mouth open wide, taking in the scene.

"Hey! Outta the way, kid!" The shout came from a teamster heading in his direction with a haul of stacked logs held together by heavy chains, each link the size of a silver dollar. A team of horses pulled the wagon, and its load slowly passed him after he stepped aside.

"'Scuse me, sir." Paul gave a nod to the teamster, who scowled in return. Paul dodged the reprimand as he spotted his group of new arrivals and took a few long steps to join them.

"You better watch yourself, big fella," said a boy who had ridden on the train with Paul. "You don't want to be gettin' in the way this early. They'll kick you right out faster than you can say 'timber.'"

Paul nodded, thinking of his parents. *Just keep my head down. Focus on my work.* He hoped he would stay out of trouble and only get attention for work done well and not work disrupted. This initial hiccup was a personal warning, and he vowed to stay out of the way from now on.

But, as it turned out, he wouldn't have to worry about it much. Within a week, Paul felt right at home. He enjoyed the daily rhythm and sounds of the camp, which blended together like music: the raucous laughter in the evenings, the clanging pots and pans before and after mealtime, the clinking of heavy chains sliding across the timber, the rhythmic back-and-forth of long, whirring saw blades. Even the swearing and spitting tobacco felt familiar, though his mother's words rang in his head each time he heard the splatter of tobacco spit. "I better not find out you're chewing that stuff, Paul Cunningham. I don't care how many of those men do it. It's a filthy habit that'll have you sleeping in the barn with the rest of the animals."

No matter how "at home" Paul felt in the woods, the stark contrast of a fourteen-year-old boy who was larger than most men made him an oddity. It seemed that every week, crew members would comment on his age or size.

"There's no way you're younger than twenty."

"Damn, boy, what did your parents feed you?"

Across the bunkhouse, someone would answer, "I don't know, but whatever it is, I'll take some."

And the laughter would commence. Paul was used to this coming from the kids around his home, but not from adults. He laughed along with them and did what his parents asked. For the first month, he put his head down and kept on swinging.

Autumn quickly faded, and Paul took to lumberjacking like a wheel takes to a wagon, and in return, he was paid well for it. Before the first real snowfall in late November, Paul made his way home for a week to bring back his wages and spend time with his parents. If the visit went well, he hoped to bring up the idea of logging more than a season at a time, maybe even stay on until the following summer.

"Paul!" Samantha shouted, waving her hand high in the air as Paul got off the train. She ran up to her son and pulled him downwards so she could hug him tightly. Finally letting him go, she took a step back to inspect her son. He was wearing the dirt of a lumberjack, and the calluses on his hands had doubled in size. "Don't wash much up there, do you?" she said. Paul puffed up and smiled at the appraisal. The dirt of a lumberjack was hard-earned, and he was clearly proud of it. She reached up to rub a smudge off his cheek. Paul blushed and pulled away as he noticed his father standing quietly behind Samantha.

"There ain't time to wash, Ma." He tried to sound annoyed, but his massive grin let her know that he was happy to see her too. Paul caught Andrew's eye and straightened up, towering a foot and a half over his father.

"Hello, Pa."

"Paul," Andrew replied. "Ride down was okay?"

Samantha watched the formal exchange between the two men. It was no longer that of a fifteen-year-old son and his father.

"Wasn't too bad." They stood still, sharing an awkward moment of silence before Paul continued. "I brought my wages back. I used a few dollars to buy some new clothes and supplies, but other than that, it's all there." Paul reached into his pocket and pulled out a wrinkled envelope. He handed it to Andrew, who took the package, opened it, and peered inside, eyes widening.

"There's a little over sixty dollars in there, Pa. They agreed to give me a little extra if I stayed on for the winter. I can do 'bout as much work as two men up there. Maybe more."

Andrew looked up at his son. For the first time, he realized how much Paul had grown during his time in the pineries. If he hadn't cradled that boy in his arms as a baby, he would have been afraid of Paul's towering size.

"How much do they pay you?" Andrew was shocked at the sum he held in his hands.

"Well, typical is twenty-five a month for a seasoned jack, but they paid the new hires twenty. After a month of showing them what I could do, they brought me up to twenty-five like the rest of the older men. I insisted on it." Paul looked from his father to his mother. "I'm really pretty good at it. I barely need any help up there." He was beaming at this point, like a child who had just taken his first steps and was searching his parents' faces for approval.

Samantha looked at the money and then at Andrew, knowing how helpful it was. This money made the winter easier to bear. It meant Andrew could restock his elixir supplies before springtime. It meant plenty of flour and lard in the cabin for the next few months. Unfortunately, it also confirmed her earlier suspicions. Her son would be heading north again. Besides an occasional visit like this one, he was essentially gone for good.

———

Paul spent the week helping around the house. He re-shoed their ox and replaced the wagon's axle again. He and his mother restocked the house pantry with the money he brought home, and he even spent an afternoon building up the firewood supply. *They'll be warm for a year*, he proudly thought to himself as he surveyed the massive pile of split pine, oak, and maple. The oak wasn't the best for quick fires, but it would do.

Even though he was busy, the week moved slowly, and Paul looked forward to getting back to camp. He sat outside his parents' home each night and watched the stars turn across the sky. Despite the peace and quiet, he could only think of swinging his ax. It was funny how such a simple thing, a piece of wood and metal, could make him feel so complete.

Just a year ago, Paul's identity would have been defined by his home and parents, but he couldn't believe how different this house felt now. In the time he had been gone, his definition of home had shifted from this building to the forests he logged. His ties to his parents, most notably his mother, were tight and essential before he left, but now he sensed he would never need them the same way as he did then.

The night around him stirred with a gust of cold air. An animal scurried from the side of the house into the protection of a nearby lilac bush, one of his mother's favorite flowers. He shivered as the wind wrapped around his neck and found its way under his shirt collar. He stood up and went inside to sleep on his old bed, which was, by now, far too small for him.

———

Over the next three years, Paul swung his ax nonstop. He moved between logging companies and towns as better offers came in, returning home every so often to visit his parents and hand off his savings.

"You can't seem to sit still, Paul," his father said during one of his visits. "Can't you just stick to one place?"

"I've gotta follow the trees, Pa. The tallest pines are getting thinned out around here, and it's gettin' harder to find 'em, you know?"

"It also means we don't see you as often," Samantha said. She sat in the wooden chair next to the iron stove as she mended one of Paul's shirts, one that would have been large enough for her to use as a blanket. She enjoyed watching Paul and Andrew together. The two had talked more comfortably in the last year or so. Andrew enjoyed hearing stories about the camps. He laughed as Paul told him about a runaway ox who had dragged a log through the camp and knocked over the cook and his pot, leaving him covered in rabbit stew.

"It's been six months since we last saw you, you know." The accusing tone in Samantha's voice was as apparent as the holes in the shirt she insisted on repairing, though Paul noticed the words were said with more longing and love than anger. She didn't look up from her lap as she weaved the worn fabric, her hands working like the agile legs of a spider.

"I know. I'm sorry, Ma. But there's just so much to do. They need me up there." He paused and took a breath, then hesitantly continued. "Come to mention it, I've been meaning to tell you that I'll be heading back tomorrow."

"Tomorrow? You only just arrived." There was surprise and pain in her voice, as if Paul had just pricked her with the needle she was holding. Andrew put another log in the stove and said nothing.

The truth was, once Paul arrived home, he had been ready to return back to the trees the very next day. He enjoyed seeing his parents, but his life was up north now, and someday it could be even farther away.

"The boy's got work to do, Sam," said Andrew, reentering the conversation. "I'm surprised you even come back at all, to be honest. You're nearly eighteen, and you're starting to make a name for yourself. Tell your mother what they call you up there."

Paul glanced at his mother, who was watching him with pleading eyes. He could tell she was longing for him to stay. To stay home longer and to stay her little child forever. But he also could tell that she knew neither of those things were possible. He looked to the ground.

"They call me Big Paul," he said.

There's my little boy, Samantha thought as she watched his cheeks flush at the nickname.

"Ha. Big Paul. You hear that? Well, it's true enough, I suppose. Not a job you can't do up there, I bet." Andrew always lit up whenever he spoke of his lumberjack son.

"Well, I can't walk the logs down the river. The best men for that job are the quick-footed, slender fellas who can spin the logs with their studded shoes. I can handle the hooks, but I'm just too heavy to run the logs." He let out a low chuckle that seemed to rattle the shutters. "I've gotten wet my fair share of times trying to learn."

"Well, if you're going to be spending more time away, I'd at least appreciate it if you could send a letter once in a while," Samantha said. "I need to know you're safe."

"Of course, Ma." Even though it sounded like a request, Paul knew a command from his mother when he heard one. A small spark of guilt flickered in his belly knowing he likely wouldn't write as much as she'd prefer.

Samantha returned to the shirt draped across her lap, and the men went back to sharing camp stories and the songs the loggers would sing at night to pass the time. She listened to Paul's deep voice accompanied by the whispering clicks of the fire.

Come on, boys, come on down
Pack your bags, get out o' town

The winter's coming, the pines are tall
We need your help if they're gonna fall

In the morning time, when the food is set
The cook will feed you with his best

Work all day till your back is wet
Steam your socks when you go to bed

Dance all night to pass the time
Nothing better than a logger's life

If you're feeling tired, your eyes are red
Rub tobacco beneath your lids

If the cold has bitten off a finger or three
Thaw 'em out with a cup of tea

When you're lying there and miss your gal
Sing her the song you know so well

Grab your pay, hold on tight
Head on down to the saloon tonight

Draw another card to pass the time
Nothing better than a logger's life

Nothing better than a logger's life

———

The next day at the train station, Samantha and Andrew found themselves saying goodbye to Paul once again. Samantha, however, had a feeling that this goodbye was different. One of these times, she may not see him again, at least not for a very, very long time.

"Remember to write," she pleaded as she gave Paul one last hug.

"I will, I will." He rolled his eyes and gave a grin to Andrew, who said his goodbye with a nod. "See you in another six months," Paul said as he reached to shake his father's hand.

"Right." Andrew kept nodding and took a step back as Paul, wearing his freshly mended clothes, turned to get on the train.

As the steam billowed and the engine slowly pulled away, Paul looked back at the shrinking silhouettes of his parents and hoped that the next six months would go as quickly for them as it would for him.

Within a month of getting back to camp, it became clear to Paul that his time in Maine was coming to an end. A day didn't go by without him hearing about lumberjacks picking up and pushing westward in search of more timber. One night after dinner, Paul sat on a stump away from the fire, sharpening his ax, while the rest of the shanty boys were gathered around the blaze. He was listening to them talk about the pine forests to the west. The stone wheel spun beneath his blade, smoothing out any imperfections on the razor edge.

"Michigan is what I heard," said one of the younger men, sipping a cup of tea from a tarnished tin cup. "Somewhere near the Muskegon River's where they said they was headed. They say the pineries there are like what Maine used to look like, only bigger."

"I heard the trees are wide as a house and four hundred feet high," chimed in another man leaning against the blacksmith shed. "Like the way they used to be here."

Paul imagined himself walking through the monstrous woods,

swinging his ax from side to side, bringing down rows of trees with each chop. He watched himself lift freshly cut logs and drink the resin that dripped from the fleshy wood. He felt it warm his body as it pumped through his veins, and he began to grow taller than the two-hundred-foot pine he had felled the previous week. He walked through forests of pine, touching their treetops with his hands the way he used to feel the blades of prairie grass alongside the road by his parents' home.

A scrape on his knuckles from the grinding stone brought him back to camp. The group of men heard Paul huff and looked over.

"You should come with us, Paul," said the man by the shed. "We could use you out there with those big pines."

Paul smiled but said nothing. His mind drifted from the pines to his parents. It would be a lot harder to visit them. *All the more reason to keep writing*, he thought. Certainly, his mother would be disappointed by the distance, but he figured that work was drying up in Maine, so the Michigan money would more than make up for it.

Paul recalled the most recent letter from his mother. "We are so looking forward to seeing you at the end of the season," she had said. Reading those words was always warming. Knowing you are loved. But there was always a cool twinge of guilt in Paul's stomach beneath the warmth. If he moved westward, those words would surely change into questions of when or if he would ever come home. The answers to those were painfully clear.

But the prospect of bigger trees was too enticing for Paul, guilt or no. He had to join.

He started working in Michigan, but in the years that followed, when the wind blew another group of men like falling maple leaves westward to just north of Wausau, Wisconsin, he raised his sails and caught the same breeze, leaving a trail of letters behind him. In their dimly lit cabin,

Samantha would read aloud the roughly written, smudged notes while Andrew listened from the opposite corner as he whittled spoons out of soft pieces of poplar. They would imagine their son, now a man in the pines, leading teams of men and shaping the countryside. Postage from Paul marked each season, but he couldn't find time to travel back to his parents. His mother's letters followed him from camp to camp. They spoke of Andrew and the weather, and they always reminded him that he could return home anytime, just as Paul thought they would. But, just like the shame he initially carried from not visiting, the requests for him to return slowly disappeared.

The only consolation that Andrew and Samantha found was by way of the tales that eventually trickled through their communities, stories and rumors of a lumberjack making his way across the United States and shaping the land as he did it. According to the tales, he stood nearly seven feet tall and was as strong as any man logging the pines. Folks from Maine all the way to Wisconsin started telling these stories about "Big Paul," who could fell a tree with just four swings of his ax. Out in the pineries, Paul would approach a tree, sizing it up and down, and lean his ax against the base while he spat into each palm and rubbed the saliva into his leathery palms, working it into a tarry paste as it mixed with the grime in his calloused fingers. Then he reached for his ax. Twisting his torso, Paul would swing twice, first down and then up, carving out a wedge in the base of the tree. With a quick hop and a couple more swings, he placed a second wedge on the opposite side of the tree, pausing only when the first sign of tipping began. He would step back and grin, calling "Timber!" as the log fell to its fate. As far as he knew, there wasn't a single lumberjack in the world that could chop as well.

And it wasn't only the tree cutting that made imaginations run wild. One night, Paul fed his crew canvasback ducks that he had cornered into some netting. The meat lasted them several days. But just as trees grow, so do the stories, and instead of fowl caught in a net, Andrew and Samantha heard word that their son tricked hundreds of migrating birds with a giant canvas which he threw to the ground to look like a pond. The ducks broke their necks landing on what they thought was a welcoming watering hole, and the men feasted like royalty for months on the juicy meat. It's funny how, after enough campfire tellings, one story can so easily turn into another.

St. Croix River, 1893

In the woods
In the swaying trees
Pine straw aroma sweet
On the back of the breeze
Moving with the waterways
I whisper to the sky
For I am
The man in the pines

"We're not burning the forests anymore. We've been our own country for a hundred years now," Paul said as he sat rosy-cheeked in his red and black plaid shirt half-unbuttoned from the neck down, his slate undershirt showing. The fabric used to be white, but white undershirts turned gray as thunderclouds with just a few days' work no matter how well you washed them. He leaned back in his chair in the corner of the bunkhouse and looked around to see who was listening. A few bearded men sat nearby, indulging his rant. Nearly twenty others were enjoying their own conversations across the crowded rectangular room. Paul went on, "That king is long dead, and this is our wood. This haul is for the new America. What's left I'm sure they'll sell to the highest bidder. But you can bet I'll be there to take these here trees down longer than any one of ya, and I'll be happy to take the money for it." Paul typically began to boast when he drank. He reached for another swig of amber whiskey.

"Don't let the boss catch you in the bottle, Big Paul. He'll have you kicked out o' camp in no time," said a man wearing red wool long johns.

"Nah. So long as I don't cause trouble, they don't mind me taking a little nip every now and then. 'Specially since I don't go to the saloons like half of y'all. Plus, I give the foreman my share of tobacco, and that keeps 'im happy enough."

Saturday evenings like this one were a relaxed affair as most of the men took Sundays off. Everyone found a spot to sit to enjoy music or storytelling, either on the benches in the middle of the room by the stove or on their beds which lined the walls of the bunkhouse. Clotheslines were tied to the bedframes and strung over the stove for wet clothes to hang like a stringer of fresh fish. It smelled just about the same with the rows of steaming wool socks hanging all night long above the hot stoves, making the bunkhouse air thick as soup. Some men sat in their long johns while others barely shed any clothing and slept in their flannels and mackinaws, only parting with their socks for the night.

Paul kicked off his boots, displaying his crimson socks damp with a day's sweat, the tip of his left big toe peeking through a small hole at the top. He slept in the corner of the bunkhouse next to a few of the Finns; the Swedes were on the other end while a hodgepodge of other nationalities filled in the middle bunks. Whether you were Norwegian, African, Indian, German, Italian, or whatever, everyone enjoyed Saturday evening in the logging camp.

As the evening wound down, a chorus of "Night, boys!" rang from the Finns all the way to the Swedes.

"Night, boys!" called the dozen men on the bunkhouse side opposite the door when everyone was in bed and the lanterns were dimmed.

"Night, boys!" the other men would sing in a rousing echo. And on and on it went, with every fourth call the entire bunkhouse rang out,

"Good night!" The chant swung back and forth like the pendulum of a grandfather clock. There weren't any particularly skilled singers in the camp, but when everyone sang off-key in unison, it blended into something full and rich.

The following week, two new loggers came into camp to fill the vacancies created by a poorly fallen tree that had left two experienced loggers with crushed legs and broken ribs. The new recruits were blond-haired Norwegians with pink cheeks and fuzzy chins. Their permanent grins sat beneath raised eyebrows as if a joke were always on the verge of delivery. The jollier of the two nudged his companion and nodded towards Paul, who was making his way across the camp. The sun was setting, and men were beginning to clean up camp before bed. The Norwegians cut, pushed, and tripped each other playfully as they sought Paul out. They found him pouring his evening tea by the bunkhouse.

"Hello there. I'm Nils, and this is Trygve," said the taller of the two.

Trygve leaned in. "You can call me Tryg."

"You must be Big Paul then?" Nils gave him a bright smile and extended a hand.

Paul took a sip from his mug, uncertain of what would come next from the comedic pair. They were like two dancing songbirds, hopping and chirping about, oblivious to their surroundings.

"I am." He leaned forward and gave the boy's hand a hard squeeze, returning the smile. Nils winced and let out a little squeak at the tall man's grip, which Paul released a moment later. "Where'd you boys come from then?"

"Lower Michigan," said Tryg, who must have been barely eighteen. He bounced with enthusiasm, and by the fresh look of the Norwegians' mackinaws and stiff boots, it was clear that this was their first year of logging.

"Seems like lots of folks are pushing more and more west. We had a few others come through last spring from your way. Headed to Minnesota, I believe." Paul kicked aside some rabbit droppings at his feet as he tried to remember precisely where those jacks went.

"That's where the trees are, so they say." Nils' eyes twinkled with excitement, and his eyebrows jumped so high they could have raised the moon.

Paul had sensed the pull further westward for some time now. He was always keen to listen for stories of bigger trees and untamed wilderness. The trees were magnets calling to the iron surging through his veins. He'd been along the St. Croix for a few years now and was beginning to feel restless. The need to move further west was making its way to the forefront of his mind.

"They also say the St. Croix has one of the finest operations in Wisconsin. That's why we came. That, and we wanted to cut trees next to Big Paul himself, of course." The two little loggers were practically glowing in the coming twilight. They followed Paul like puppies starved for attention as he walked towards the fire by the other loggers, and now he was starting to understand the enthusiasm that Tryg and Nils wore. It was him, not the trees, that excited them.

Their other words also echoed in his ears.

St. Croix has one of the finest operations.

It always seemed that the moment a logging camp was called "fine" or "outstanding" or "the best around" was the moment it started slowing down. *Maybe that's the nature of it? Once you name something a success, you've ruined it.*

At twenty-three years old, Paul didn't altogether mind being a role model for the kids, but the thought that these forests were drying up made him uneasy, anxious even. An image of a land with nothing but tree stumps flashed before him, and a warm tingling crawled up the back of his neck as a stab of nausea sunk into his belt. He blinked the scene away. *Nah, I'll be logging until I die, and there'll always be more for me to cut.*

"Any of you boys hear word from Minnesota? What do things look like over there?" Paul asked.

A few eyebrows lifted and some ears perked up at this.

"You will not be leaving us, will you, Bon Jean?" A man with sandy hair, a thick beard, and chapped, smiling cheeks beamed at Paul.

"Maybe I am, and maybe I'm not." Paul smirked at the lone French Canadian in the camp. "And what did I say about that name, Joe?"

Joe was nearly as well-known in camp as Paul for his strength and height. He had come down from Ontario the previous fall, and, shortly after meeting Paul Cunningham, Joe had told him he looked like a braver, taller version of his cousin, Jean.

"Believe me, it is a worthy comparison," Joe said.

"Well, it'll take more convincing than that," Paul said, giving him a skeptical glance. "And your silly nickname is becoming a running joke. My name is Paul or Cunningham or nothing."

Even as he said it, the foreman called from across the clearing, "Hey, Bon Jean, good work yesterday!"

Paul cringed, and his irritation doubled in size. "I'm not going to win this battle, am I?" It seemed that the men around camp thought the rhyming was catchy. The old words of his mother rang through his head. *Just put your head down and swing your ax.*

Sensing the undercurrent of frustration, Joe added, "I only use that name to compliment you, my friend. And I would be saddened to see you leave."

"Maybe you would be sad," Paul said, pausing to drain the rest of his cup, "but if I do, I think you'd agree with my decision. You're just like me. When there is better logging to be had elsewhere, ya go. When the best trees are gone, so am I." With that, he walked over to set his empty cup in the dish bin, his heavy boots clunking as he walked. Then he bent down to tie his laces. "Get some rest, boys. We've got a lot of trees to clear tomorrow."

He left the young Norwegians and the Frenchman chattering behind him as he stepped outside the camp boundary into the cool night air. Turning back, Paul saw the soft glow of the lanterns shining through the bunkhouse windows. It was refreshing to leave the musty air of the bunks, which could be terribly oppressive. Like being covered in heavy, wet sand.

No matter the season, Paul liked to take one last walk in the dark before calling it a night. Winter was best, of course. No one else dared come out in the cold. He was completely alone. Alone with the drifts of snow muffling the sounds and covering him in silence. But now, in the autumn night, he walked into the woods, deeper and deeper, following the fresh, sweet scent of the pines and listening to the scraping of his feet on the dirt beneath him.

When a tall white pine has just been cut, the sap stains the skin on your hands, and the aroma of the sap lingers for a week or so. The smell is refreshing as you wash your face in a fresh spring bubbling from the side of a hill. On these fall nights, Paul would walk until he stood blanketed in the air of the fallen trees, listening to the night forest. The men in the camp may need their rest, but the forest never slept. Owls hooted to one another, and mice rustled and scratched as they stocked up food for winter, doing their best to stay hidden from the nighttime hunters who silently moved about in the darkness. Occasionally, the howl of a wolf would ride on the wind as a reminder that humans were not the only rulers of the north.

Wolves were well-known to stalk loggers who wandered about in the dark. Once or twice, Paul had even crossed paths with small packs of the lurking, toothy animals. But they were smart, and it didn't take them too long to size up the moose of a man wielding a dangerous weapon. Paul recalled a logger named Louie Blanchard he'd recently met when passing through the Chippeway. Louie spoke of a logger who had been stripped to his bones by the wolves, with nothing left but the feet in his boots.

A few times, the wolves got pretty close to Paul, snarling and threatening to bite, but he was able to scare them off with a few massive swings of his ax. He thought fondly of these private adventures as he moved through the darkness, listening to scurrying critters around him. The mice and the raccoons. The shuffling feet of a nearby porcupine searching for the right tree to call home. *You're gonna have to walk for a while,* Paul thought as he recalled his haul for the day.

His thoughts drifted to the time he last saw his parents. It had already been a year. With his push westward, the increasing distance between them meant less frequent visits.

He never admitted it to any of the other jacks, but he missed seeing his parents and it was hard to think of them. Paul enjoyed coming home to share his exploits with his father and hand him the money. He'd tell tales of the practical jokes loggers would play on each other and describe every tree he cut down. It was in these brief moments that Paul felt the paternal approval he had always been seeking. And as for his mother, it was in Samantha's presence that he could shrink down and let pretenses fall to the wayside. Just the thought of her relaxed the taut muscles running from Paul's neck to his shoulders.

His drifting mind was called back to the forest by a start-and-stop pitter-patter behind him, a sound so subtle that he nearly missed it. Paul turned and looked directly into the eyes of a rabbit. It twitched its nose and hopped out between the tree stumps and nearby piles of discarded branches and cut treetops. The rabbit didn't look like anything special. In the moonlight, Paul could see the dirty gray fur, a lighter patch of gray beneath the chin, and the faint, rust-colored hairs on the back of the neck. He stared at it for a long time, perplexed by the courage of the rabbit. If it hadn't been looking straight at him, he could have sworn it hadn't seen him. Then, to Paul's further surprise, it made a few hops closer, its whiskers flicking up and down like dancing pine needles. It shifted its body and nestled down in a cushion of long, dry needles, gazing directly at him. The two sat like that, frozen. Crickets chirped in the distance, and farther away, a long, mournful howl of a wolf rang out.

"Well, what can I do for ya, little fella?" Paul curled his lips into a wide, toothy grin, amused by the rabbit and its domesticated behavior. "Just passing through? Don't see many of your kind around camp these days, do we?"

In fact, any rabbit seen was a rabbit shot and cooked. Rabbit stew was a favorite dish after a long day of hard work, and you knew the cook had prepared a good meal when the only conversation at dinner was smacking lips and slurping gulps followed by a groan or a belch. No words found their way to the table when rabbit was the main course.

He took a step closer to the furry little creature, and it stood its ground. Paul looked around, knowing no one else was there but hoping someone happened to see what was unfolding.

"Alright, little guy, if you're gonna stay, so will I." He sat down on the nearest stump, facing his new acquaintance. The base of the tree was a good four feet in diameter and had been sawed level to the ground, probably by the Finns, not chopped by him.

Paul was thankful for the seat. He set his right elbow on his thigh and rested his chin on his palm, his thumb and forefinger spreading across his thick mustache and circling down his stubbled chin. It was a calm night, and the moonlight filtered through the clouds, lying like a blanket on the distant treetops. A thick fog was rolling in like a lulling surf on a rocky shore, enveloping the stumps and eventually circling Paul's ankles. He had seen fog like this before on the Great Lakes of the north but couldn't recall how close he was to any body of water now. After a couple of slow blinks and a deep sigh, he closed his heavy eyelids on the dark, glistening eyes of the rabbit and opened them to meet the warm, welcoming, chestnut eyes of his mother.

"Hello, son. How I've missed you." She didn't speak the words as much as exhale them. She was standing in the same dark woods, holding the rabbit in her arms. The animal continued to watch Paul.

Paul was drunk with confusion. He was thankful to see his mother, but he couldn't put the pieces together. "What're ya doing here, Ma? Where's Pa? Is he with you?" In these woods, miles away from home, he couldn't comprehend how she stood before him now. His stomach began to flutter uneasily, like the logs rolling on the river. "Ma, what's goin' on?"

"Paul, I wanted to tell you in person, but it's been so hard to find you." She paused to gather her courage. "Your father and I got sick. I don't think we'll get better, and I don't think we'll make it to next spring when you return." All of this she said with a smile, gently petting the rabbit behind its ears.

"What do you mean you got sick? How did you get here?"

"We are so proud of how you've grown." She chuckled to herself and added, "It looks like you're still growing. Those pants are too short for you."

He looked down at the gap between his cuffs and the tops of his loosely laced boots.

"You'll need to move further west," she continued. "You have work to do in the harder country in northern Minnesota. When you get there, try to open your heart. Try to see what she will show you."

The fog was climbing above his knees to his belt now, billowing like a thunderhead and dimming his vision. Wolves howled in the distance. The fog choked his words and clouded his mind. He saw tanned faces of dark-haired men and women walking across the land. They paddled canoes across lakes and tracked caribou through the forests. They danced and sang in high voices to a rhythm that matched his heartbeat. Suddenly, Paul was surrounded by towering piles of logs. Beneath his feet, water began to rise and curled into a building tidal wave. The wall of water pulled itself up like a snake preparing to strike, and it fell onto the crowds of people. It pushed the fog through the stacks of timber, lifting the people and logs high into the air, washing them all away. He felt his legs stretch and his muscles lengthen as his body reached towards the clouds, and with a loud *crack*, Paul jerked his head up and opened his eyes.

He clutched his chest as he struggled for breath in the cold air. His canvas pants felt stiff against his skin, and his plaid shirt, soaked with sweat, clung to his body. Paul was lying on his side, a broken branch beneath him. His head was pounding and spinning. The images, the faces, the rabbit, his mother's words, all swirled around him mercilessly until finally they began to ebb away like receding floodwaters. Once they vanished, Paul was left with blind apprehension. The dream had dissolved, but anxiety remained. He felt as if he were standing on a lake of ice he knew was too thin to hold him.

He stood up and brushed off the loose needles and dirt clinging to his shirt. Then, shaking the pain and confusion from his head, he made his way back to the snoring camp. It took Paul an hour to fall asleep, leaving little time until daybreak, and the hint of sleep he did get was restless and uneasy.

When he woke, the images of the night before spun in his mind like a whirlpool. Most of his mother's words were fading no matter how hard he tried to remember them. Only a few remained. He buttoned his shirt for the day and tightened his suspenders. *What happened last night? What did Ma say? I'm sure everything's fine. It was just a dream.*

He looked to the cuffs of his pants and saw that they were inching above the top laces of his boots. His shirt was taut as a deer hide. Sure enough, by mid-morning, he split the back of his flannel while swinging his ax. The fabric separated straight down his spine with an abrasive shredding sound. But there was nothing like a good day of work to get his mind back on track after such a strange night, so Paul's ax continued to swiftly bury deep into the trees, which fell like blades of grass. After the trees fell, his muscles pumped with endless strength as he dragged log after log to the teams of oxen awaiting their next load to haul away.

Before he knew it, that night in the woods quickly moved to the back of his memory, and his full attention returned to logging. Nothing made him happier. He rarely needed a hand from any of the men on the crew, who could now call him Brave Paul Bon Jean as much as they liked. Paul welcomed the nicknames and the stories that spread. The rumors built space between him and the other loggers, which led to more freedom to log on his own.

Even the little things he did became camp legend, and he took joy in it. Paul had dug a trench one morning to divert a spring and, with the help of some strategically placed stones, saplings, and clay, had made a small pool that could be used for bathing and washing. *Let them think I can carve the waterways and dig the lakes. If they want me to be Big Paul, then so be it.*

When the letters came around that month, he watched as the

foreman, a big-bellied, ghostly pale man who went by the name Birch, called out names and men came forward, one by one, to grab their mail.

"That it?" Paul called to Birch after he passed out the last letter. He'd been hoping to see something from home. He couldn't explain it, but even a short note would have set him at ease. The images from the dream were all gone besides that of his mother cradling a rabbit and a few words she said, but the episodes of panic and nausea came in unpredictable waves. It was rare to have more than three months pass without hearing from his mother, and it had been at least five since the last letter. The foreman noticed the worried expression on his face.

"That's it, Paul. You expecting somethin'?"

"Nah," Paul said. He thought of writing to his parents but stifled the urge. "Just wonderin'." He stood up and grabbed his things, ready for the day of work that lay ahead. *I'm being silly, that's all. They're fine. I'll write 'em soon as I get a chance.*

But every so often in the weeks that followed, as the damp woodland air gave way to crisp breezes, he swore he saw that same rabbit from his mother's arms darting just beyond his sight. With every glimpse of the rabbit, he thought of his mother, and Minnesota, and the only words that stayed with him from that foggy night in the woods: "Try and see what she will show you."

To Hinckley, 1893

The stars aren't the miraculous part.
It's the darkness between them.
What lies out there in that dark forest?
The deepest sea?
The void that is nothing and everything?
The dark spaces of the sky that get lost each day in the light of a single star?

"Paul! Bon Jean! Post for ya. From Michigan."

Fall had come early with cool temperatures and falling leaves, and now it looked like winter was following suit. The first snow arrived in the beginning of October, and the ground was hardening quickly. *At least we don't have to battle in the mud much longer*, Paul thought as he walked toward the foreman.

"Big Paul, I don't know what you're eatin', but ya just keep gettin' taller and taller," Birch said.

Besides handling the mail, Birch's duties included working with the barons to make sure production was on task and taking reports from the cruisers, the men who scouted the next possible logging locations. Paul didn't care for the foreman much but felt he could read him well enough, and from Birch's recent sour attitude, Paul knew the logging would be getting harder, which meant the time to leave the St. Croix area was quickly approaching. Most likely, he'd be making his way over to the pineries of Minnesota where the sawmills and lumberyards were picking up steam.

"I don't measure myself every day, sir, but my boots do seem to be gettin' tight again."

Paul took the beige envelope and tore it open as he turned away. He felt guilty that he hadn't taken the time to write to his parents, but was thankful, nonetheless, to get a letter from home. As Paul looked back at the envelope, he was puzzled by the unfamiliar handwriting. Tossing the envelope aside, he unfolded the note, which was dated the previous month, and began to read.

Dear Mr. Paul Cunningham,

It is with a heavy heart that I write to inform you that your parents, Andrew and Samantha Cunningham, became ill with the fever this past August. Your father could not survive the early stages of the illness and went to meet our Lord quickly. Your mother seemed to improve, but began to have fits and, sadly, also passed away. While she was still able to speak, she asked to write to you and remind you of her love.

As you know, they had few possessions. Their belongings (e.g., wagon, assorted tools, home, a single oxen) have been left to you. If you are unable to collect them, please reply to this letter and I can liquidate them for you and return the money, minus fees for service.

I am deeply sorry for your loss.

Regards,

Thomas Blakely, Esq.

The words burned on the page. *Fever? Passed away?* Paul's eyes began to sting, and the letters blurred as he read the message over and over. Visions of his mother danced in his head with her kind smile and warm embrace, fragile in his big arms. The once forgotten dream rushed back into his memory. He was struck by a flash of his mother standing in front of him, holding the rabbit in her arms, and staggered back a few paces, catching himself before he fell. He heard more of her words this time.

"Your father and I got sick...You'll need to move further west...Try and see what she will show you."

"Bon Jean, are you alright?" While all the other crew members knew the custom of giving space and silence when hard news came, the fair-haired French Canadian with socks pulled high above his calves was either oblivious or ambivalent to this custom and quickly came to Paul's side, placing a hand on the middle of the giant's back. "Come, *ami*. Sit down."

He led Paul like a child leading a dazed buffalo over to the edge of the main camp and sat him down at an empty table. Paul's face was red and his eyelashes glistened, but he was tense and quiet.

To Joe, Paul looked taller whenever his emotions ran high. Whether it was anger, childish joy, or sorrow, like now, the energy radiating out of Paul also seemed to seep back in and fill his frame with each yell, laugh, or in this case, measured breath. Joe knew his friend had grown at least an inch taller since he had met him. The Frenchman had to tilt his head back, nearly to the sky, to look Paul in the face.

Joe thought of the first time he'd met Paul, in the St. Croix Valley along the banks of a log-jammed tributary to the big river. The lumberjacks needed the rivers almost as much as they needed the trees, and that tributary was filled with timber from the winter season. Swampers were running across the timber, poking and prodding with their hooks trying to free up the jam. But they may as well have been trying to corral the clouds. Not a single log moved beneath their feet. Paul had laughed at the swampers' futile efforts and, from the shore, called out, "Looks like ya need some help, eh boys? Watch out there then!"

Paul then grabbed a long, slender log resting on the banks, thick as his thigh, and hoisted it up over his head. He slammed the end of the log down into the front of the jam. The mass of logs crunched and bobbed but refused to give. Joe had watched as Paul, looking larger than any lumberjack he'd ever seen, laughed and jumped to grab the free end of the log, which was suspended a good fifteen feet in the air. After he wrapped his arms around the bark, he heaved downward, and the trees at the base exploded upwards and sent a shockwave through the logjam. The retreating swampers returned and quickly began digging their cleats into the trees as the jam started to free up and make its way into the big St. Croix. Paul had looked to the river with pride as it emptied like a spilled bottle of whiskey. Then he let out a booming laugh before turning to get back to work.

But tonight, all joy was wiped clean from Paul's face as he sat at the table, looking at the ground.

"Do you want to talk?" Joe knew the answer but needed to ask.

Paul didn't respond. He simply sat, shoulders rising and falling with each breath.

The camp began to resume its normal pace, and the usual cacophony picked back up. The blacksmith, whose job it was to make sure all the blades in camp were sharp, was working Paul's ax back and forth across the grinding stone, throwing sparks to the ground. Suddenly, a shovel was tossed toward his shack and knocked with a loud clang against a neighboring row of axes waiting to be sharpened. The noise shook Paul from his unfocused stare. "Huh? No, I'll be fine." He rose, cleared his throat, then walked over to retrieve his ax, leaving Joe behind.

"I'll take that if ya don't mind." Paul yanked the ax from the blacksmith. "You know I do that myself." The blacksmith cowered at the rebuke. All eyes in the camp were on Paul as he walked up to the foreman, the only sounds the stamping feet of horses in the distance.

"Sir, I'm puttin' in my notice. I'll work through the end of the week, but then I'm done."

And with heavy steps that rattled the shovels and axes in the blacksmith's shack and sent vibrations up the vertebrae of the foreman, Paul walked off to find the largest trees he could, intent on bringing them all down one swift swing at a time.

———

A week later, Paul was moving further west, crossing from Wisconsin into Minnesota. He traveled by foot over field, stream, and through forests. In the journey's solitude, he spent most of his time thinking about his father and mother.

If there was one thing Paul had learned from Andrew, it was how to build a wall. His father was a determined man, almost as much as his mother, but what she had in openness and thoughtful glances, he had in stoic responses and guarded emotions. The day he had handed Paul the ax was the most direct show of affection he had ever offered his son. Paul looked to the ax in his hands. The wood shined in the areas where his palms did their work, and the blade was sharp and slick with oil. He'd grown so much since the day his father had given it to him that his hands now dwarfed the handle and made it look as if he were wielding a hatchet. The ax had once been heavy in his arms, needing a deliberate effort to lift. Now he often forgot he was holding it.

Maybe his father had a hard upbringing, or maybe his walls were built brick by brick out of necessity to provide for his family. Regardless, Andrew's lack of affection didn't bother Paul all that much. In fact, he recognized the strength required to be an island and tried to embody it. The less emotion Paul showed, the less dependent he felt on others.

Besides, most of the logging men weren't there to make friends. A good portion of them were likely running from something. Whether it be the law, debt, or a woman, lumberjacks were islands unto themselves, and the last thing anyone wanted was to run from one problem into the maw of another.

Paul thought back to a night in the bunkhouse before he had left for Michigan. He had been lying down, staring at the sagging mattress of the bunk above him, listening to a toothless jack with one sunken, blind eye yammering on about all the women that had troubled him in his life.

"I swear to you, when I boarded the train to make my way north from Detroit," the man's toothless grin spat with every other syllable, "I looked out the window to my left to see Miss Mary Anne, pretty as a spring rain with hair soft as summer corn silk, crying at the window for me to stay and marry her that week. Tears were streaming like God had sent a second flood to wipe away all you sinners. And from the other side of the train, through the window to my right, here comes the fury of the devil himself, little Sally Gibson, throwing fists like stones and speaking of betrayal and theft, of which I am totally and completely innocent, I thank you very much. Between you and me, she was just sore that I couldn't dedicate my life to her when my calling was elsewhere. It wasn't my fault she convinced her daddy to buy me a new set of clothes and a horse, which I had to sell due to the fact I was a'leavin.'"

Paul had glanced around the bunkhouse, where most of the men sat wide-eyed and still as statues, fully engrossed in the story, completely lost to the utterly impossible idea that this gangly, toothless fella who was more weasel than man had convinced not one, but two beautiful women to fall for him.

In the logging camps, entertainment was entertainment, but for Paul, the thought of complicating his life with the uncharted and potentially dangerous aspect of love seemed not only unnecessary but also foolish. Therefore, he avoided the risk altogether and steered clear of the saloons and any other temptation. The previous summer on the St. Croix, several of the men in his crew frequently left the camps to head to town for gambling and companionship not offered in the bunkhouses.

"Why don't you come with us, Bon Jean? I bet you're a fine card player," one of the swampers had called.

"Yeah, Paul, we'll gladly take some money off your hands. There's plenty of lonely women down there I'm sure would love to meet ya too, eh boys?" said a fellow jack as the others laughed.

"Why don't ya keep 'em company for me, then? I'm fine right here," Paul said, plenty happy to be logging by day and laughing by night, keeping his relationships on the other side of the wall his father had taught him to build. The closest he would get to one of his fellow jacks was just close enough to slip some molasses in their shoes while they were sleeping so they'd have a sticky surprise in the morning, a classic lumberjack trick. *Let 'em have their poker and their women,* Paul thought.

Paul nodded to himself as he walked through a grove of sugar maples, passing a stray walnut tree. *A new state. New trees. Simple enough. I don't need any relationships complicating that, new or old.* He picked up a few black walnuts and crushed the shells in his hand as if they were brittle as dried leaves. He flicked away the shards of hard shell and popped the meat into his mouth, enjoying the earthy, sweet flavor.

After he crossed into Minnesota, Paul noticed the subtle changes in scenery, the slight rise in elevation, and the cooler air as he moved farther north. The temperature swung like sleeping breaths, with a deep inhale each night as the world began to freeze followed by a warm breath out each day as the sun tried to fight off the inevitable, looming winter. There were big animals in these forests too. One morning, he spooked a small herd of caribou and was astonished at their majestic antlers, which reached upwards like long-fingered hands toward the sky. In the years to come, he would run into his fair share of bears, moose, wolves, and mountain lions as well. For the most part, the animals seemed to acknowledge Paul with the same regard they would give one of their own, pausing to recognize the other's presence, then going about their business of preparing for the constant inevitability of snow.

Paul first traveled north towards the shores of Duluth. He was in search of some place he could escape to and, just possibly, make a little money to pay for lodging. He walked through the busy shipping town resting on the shores of Lake Superior. The homes, mills, and factories were huddled together on a steep, rocky slope that bowed in submission to the oceanic lake. Paul noticed a row of boarding houses for the harbor and mill workers that was built into a hillside. It looked like just the sort of place he could afford, assuming there was a job for him in the harbor.

Paul asked around and was able to find the landlord for one of the buildings.

"Sure, as long as you can pay, you can stay. I can set you up with one of the crews in the harbor if you'd like. Big man like you, they'd love to have you down there."

"That'd be fine. I appreciate it."

The landlord started leading Paul up a narrow staircase toward a small room on the third floor. The stale air and dingy light made the passageway feel like a coffin. The wooden floor moaned so much with each of Paul's heavy footsteps that by the time they reached the second-floor landing, the sounds beneath their feet had become loud and concerning. The landlord stopped and cast a troubled look to Paul's feet, then to his, and finally back up to the giant's bearded, weather-worn face.

"Maybe I should find you a room on the first floor."

———

Before Paul knew it, a month had passed. The deaths of his parents pushed his mind into a blurry snowstorm. He spent his days in the harbor, heaving logs into large piles to be sorted for either shipping or loading onto the railways, which were being used more and more for hauling. Besides a polite "thank you" or an affirming nod, Paul didn't speak to a single soul for the remainder of his time in Duluth unless it was absolutely necessary.

The biting cold finally eased in mid-January, giving a respite to the men working outside who fought daily to keep the frostbite from their noses, fingertips, and toes. Large sheets of ice heaved up and down in the harbor as Paul walked through a gentle flurry of snowflakes to the Beltline Railway, a shaky, loud trolley car that moved to a high enough point for passengers to look out over the harbor. He tried to squeeze into the train car every Sunday when he wasn't working. It was on one of those rides where Paul learned, much to his chagrin, that somehow his French-Canadian nickname had arrived in Minnesota before he did. However, like the landscape and the people who inhabited it, the name had changed as well.

A young boy, maybe five years old or so, bundled up in a black wool hat and jacket was tugging at his mother's sleeve and staring in Paul's direction. "Hey, Ma," he said.

"Yes, dear?" the mother answered without looking at her son. She was gazing out the window to the moody waters of the big lake. Snow had been falling intermittently for a week or so, and the lake seemed to reflect the sullen faces of the townspeople.

"I think that's the big lumberjack Dad was talking about. What's his name? Bunyan?" The boy pointed to the man sitting behind them. His mom, now turning around to glance at Paul, who looked like an ox packed in a whiskey barrel on the small train car, pushed her son's hand down.

"It's not polite to point, Henry." She gave a nervous but polite smile to Paul and shifted closer to the window, pulling Henry to her side tightly with her arm over his shoulder.

"I think it's him, Ma," the boy whispered, then peered over his shoulder when his mother wasn't looking and gave Paul a wave.

Paul tipped his head to the boy.

When it came down to it, he didn't mind how his name continued to drift further from Cunningham. Admittedly, the rumors about his strength were flattering, but the less the folks knew about him and his past, including his real last name, the better. *I'm strongest workin' on my own,* he thought. *And it's easier to do so when folks don't know who you really are.*

By the end of January, Paul began to tire of the work in the harbor and made arrangements to migrate back into the trees to start logging again. At first, he didn't care where he logged or who it was for, but over the next few months, Paul jumped from camp to camp, following the trail to what he saw as the answer to his logging prayers. There was word of a small town southwest of Duluth called Hinckley that was growing fast and filling up with lumberyards. Every time the name entered his mind, Paul felt a flutter in his stomach and goose bumps covered his arms.

He couldn't explain it, but he knew he needed to get to Hinckley and find a company that could feed him a diet of tall trees and steady work. Paul was spending less and less time thinking about his parents and more time looking forward to swinging his ax. As the days continued to lengthen, the weight of his parents' deaths lifted too. The sunny days, though few and far between, seemed a little warmer and brighter, and the time had come to return to real work. Spring was still a month or so away, but when it came, the ice would release the logs waiting to make their way downstream. Plenty of men would exchange winter logging jobs to farm for the summer, which would leave more work for Paul.

Paul walked into Hinckley, Minnesota, from the north with the sun halfway up the baby blue sky on his left. The town was awake on this rare warm winter day. People of all ages were venturing out of their homes and businesses to soak up the fleeting sunshine, knowing all too well that more snow was inevitable. In the north, winter never wanders too far. When the cold starts to release its grip, everyone, no matter how old, feels fifteen pounds lighter and optimism blows through doorways and windows. It's easier to smile when the long winter begins to yield to springtime.

Kids were running through the streets, laughing and kicking puddles from the melting piles of snow. Even Paul couldn't help but laugh at the sight of the carefree children running past him as he moved through town, passing hotels, restaurants, and a railroad depot. His feet kept leading him south towards the large lumber mill at the end of the long dirt road.

There was a good chance of running into an owner or manager of the mill with all this activity. He stepped over a mountain of wet snow and walked over the railroad tracks in a single step, making his way to the warehouse of the Brennen Lumber Mill. A mill by the tracks was just the sort of place where Paul would likely find year-round work. As he walked into the building, he reached up toward the broad, rectangular sign above the doorway and ran his fingers across the white letters spelling "Brennen."

Mr. Brennen was talking to several crew members inside the massive wooden building when a shadow fell across his face. He looked up to see the shape of a man eclipse the light in the doorway, then watched the man take a step forward and scan the room. Spotting the group of men, the giant moved toward them. Everyone's attention was on Paul as he approached Mr. Brennen, looming above him like the Colossus of Rhodes.

"Excuse me, sir. Are you the one in charge at this mill?" Paul could tell by the man's spotless shirt and pressed pants that he was not one of the logging men.

"I am. I'm Patrick Brennen. You the big guy I keep hearing stories about from over in the St. Croix?"

"I suppose that's me. I go by Paul mostly." He extended his hand, large as a bear's paw, to Mr. Brennen. Mr. Brennen was middle-aged, with deep creases around his eyes and a kind face. Paul sensed that, in spite of his gentle demeanor, Mr. Brennen was likely a shrewd businessman to have such a profitable lumber company and, therefore, was someone who didn't like to beat around the bush. Mr. Brennen straightened his wool coat and cap and looked up into Paul's face. Paul's eyes were a cool, dark gray, like the sky after a storm has passed.

Paul continued, "Cunningham's my given name if you must know, but lots of people 'round here've been calling me Bunyan more recently. I'm looking for a job, sir. I'm hoping to find and fell the tallest pines in Minnesota, and I'm hoping to do it for you. If you'll let me, that is."

Mr. Brennen and the other men wore surprised looks on their faces, clearly stunned by the sudden appearance of such a massive lumberjack. Paul went on, "I should tell you, I tend not to swing a cant hook since I'm too big for running the logs on the river when the thaw comes." His tone was serious and determined.

Mr. Brennen noticed the tall man wince when he gave his real name, as if he were removing the bandage on a fresh wound. He wasn't quite sure what to think of Paul, but he'd be a fool not to accept a man like this on his crew. With the light from the doorway bouncing off Paul's shoulders, he looked nearly twice as wide as Mr. Brennen was tall, and his head seemed to graze the rafters of the warehouse. The decision to hire was made the minute Paul walked in.

"You'll get paid just the same as all the others. Starting is twenty dollars a month, but if you show me you're worth it, you'll make thirty. Meal and board included. I don't accept any funny business. If you like the drink and it disrupts your work, you'll be out of camp faster than you can call 'timber.'"

"That sounds fair, sir. I'd like to start as soon as possible if it's alright with ya."

"I think we can arrange that. Jeremiah here oversees inventory and will get you set up with the shanty boys. The foreman there will let you know where we're logging, and then you'll go from there. The cruisers just came back with some good word on a few separate acreages with more board feet than we can count. Get ready to be busy, Cunningham."

"Thank you, sir. I won't let you down." Paul winced again at the sound of his last name. He had meant to keep that information to himself. *Too late now,* he thought. He waited until Mr. Brennen finished addressing the other men, then walked with Jeremiah out of the mill to get his orders.

"Paul!" Mr. Brennen shouted from the dim light of the mill. A single ray from a distant window shone on Paul, specs of dust dancing in the dandelion glow. "We're in the middle of an evergreen gold rush here in the north. I'm looking forward to seeing how much you can dig."

Paul nodded, then turned to catch up to Jeremiah. It was spring, and his bones ached to feel the blade of his ax cut through the bark and deep into the pith of the trees.

Two weeks back into a bustling logging camp and Paul felt his strength sprouting like the spring ferns. He usually liked to work alone, running off ahead of the crew and bringing down trees twice as fast as the others, but he had been paired by the foreman with another lumberjack, a Finnish fellow named Otto Walta, who wore a long, fiery red mustache that curled upwards like a wild grapevine climbing a trellis. It was a rare occasion when Paul didn't mind working with someone else, but the two fit well together. Otto was a strong man who could keep up with Paul without too much complaint. He had spent his fair share of time exploring and homesteading the north and was familiar with the way trees fell. Unlike Paul, who preferred a double-bit ax, Otto carried a long crosscut saw. He could bring down a tree faster than any man, save Paul. He was quick on his feet too, which came in handy not only in keeping up with Paul's long steps, but also with dodging the occasional large pine that decided to leap back at him when it was falling.

"I can't believe ya prefer that thing to an ax." Paul pointed at Otto's freshly sharpened saw that lay against a log near the center of camp. The two were taking turns warming their hands by the open fire. "I've seen quite a few fellas meet their Maker with one of those things. They just couldn't get away from the tree quick enough before she'd jumped back at 'em like a mountain lion."

Otto laughed, his mustache waving up and down like the wings of a phoenix. "I always have a plan of escape if the tree decides to bite back. So, you cut your way, and I'll cut mine, my friend."

Together, the two men could clear a grove quick as could be. They'd take the pines for the mills and cedars for shingling the houses back in

Hinckley. When the timber cruisers came back with word on where to log next, the foreman came to Paul and Otto first.

"You boys get up there by first light tomorrow and get us started. Be sure to clear a road so we can haul the logs out." The foreman was fully aware of the luxury he had with these two on his team. Paul figured a bonus would be coming his way as Brennen's mill would likely be the leading producer of lumber now that he and Otto were in full swing and the winter was finally giving way to warmer weather.

Even in the spring, however, the cold still waged its losing battle each night. As the sun set, anything that thawed during the day, including the roads, would freeze up only to melt into a muddy soup by the next midday. This, in turn, made for messy, and sometimes dangerous, hauling of timber. It was the only thing that could slow down Mr. Brennen's crew.

Paul and Otto were walking back to camp for dinner on a particularly muddy day when Otto leaned over and gestured toward a large carriage parked near the canteen. "Did you hear? Mr. Brennen's daughter has come to visit the camp. They say she's as beautiful as a sunrise."

Paul glanced up as he pushed past a pile of branches, kicking up a few songbirds and a cottontail. The carriage was still. The two horses harnessed in front patiently shifted their weight back and forth, waiting for the signal to move.

"No, I didn't hear nothin'. Are you looking for sunrises these days, Otto?" Paul smiled at his companion.

"I never pass up the chance to watch the sun set or rise, but I wouldn't dare get close to Mr. Brennen's daughter. The man would have me chained to a log and sent down the river." Paul knew this to be true. Mr. Brennen was known to fire any man on the spot who was caught disrespecting him, his business, or his family.

"And rightfully so. Just the thought of a fine lady mixing with a woodsman like yourself would frighten most fathers." Paul nudged his friend in the ribs. Otto let out a mixture of laughter and a grunt from the powerful jab, which felt like a small tree stump had hit him in the side.

Their conversation was interrupted by some shouting and a loud whinny from a nearby horse. One of the horses helping pull a heavy load of timber on a skid sleigh had slipped in the slough of ice and mud along the road and fallen to its knees. The animal was throwing its head and calling out violently in panic.

Several men were running now, hurrying to try and pull the frightened horse up to its feet. The longer the sleigh sat, the more likely the rails would sink into the mud and freeze in place with the dropping temperatures. The longer the horse was down, the more likely it would get hurt. A broken leg meant a dead horse, and a dead horse was a huge cost. This was the risk of using the sleighs in the spring, but the benefits almost always outweighed the risks. Almost.

While a group of men hopelessly pulled the horse by her reins, a few others began pushing her from behind. Unfortunately, this startled the partner horse, who kicked her front legs high into the air in alarm, ultimately slipping and falling to her side as well.

"Hey! Someone release those horses from that skid!" shouted the foreman. It would be his fault if these horses ended up dead, and the money would come out of his pocket. It might even cost him his job.

Men were slipping and falling in the mud around the horses, adding to the frenzy. Finally, one of the lumberjacks pulled himself up using the haunch of the horse closest to him and worked his fingers on the leather straps connecting the animals to the haul of timber. His hands fiddled clumsily on the mud-covered bindings.

"It's too slippery! I think it's starting to freeze. Darn thing's jammed or something! Ah!" The horse he was leaning on tried to stand, but fell again, lunging in the man's direction and slamming him back to the ground as he let out a string of mud-covered expletives.

More men pulled the reins from the front, but the necks of the horses just stretched in protest, and the beasts showed their bared teeth clinging to the bits of the harnesses. Even the onlookers were straining and clenching their jaws, willing the horses, willing anything, to move. The situation was quickly moving from chaotic to disastrous.

Without thinking, Paul began running, leaving Otto behind. He scooped up a rope that was lying on a nearby stump as he raced to the animals. The ground shook and the chains on the sleigh rattled as Paul's thundering footsteps slid to a halt in front of the team of horses.

All of the men backed away as he wound the rope around the front legs of the sleigh and grabbed the reins from the logger holding them. The man looked stunned at the sudden appearance of Paul, who seemed to radiate electric adrenaline.

"Come on, girls. Don't fight. Don't break a leg on me." Speaking to himself just as much as the two anxious animals, Paul began gathering the ropes with the reins in his hands. The horses looked at him with sideways glares, wide-eyed and frightened.

He drove his feet into the ground, one in front of the other, and turned his back to the sleigh that was now sinking in the mud like a ship's anchor, then swung the reins and rope over his shoulder. He began pulling with Samsonian strength. The veins in his neck and temples rose like flooding rivers. The ground around his feet seemed to quake as, slowly, the horses began to rise and the sleigh started to move. Paul was screaming through clenched teeth, and his face was as blood red as his flannel. Just as suddenly as the horses fell, they jumped to their feet and stumbled into an awkward trot, hauling the load of logs and picking up speed. The driver hurried back onto the bench atop the sleigh and grabbed the reins tossed by Paul. With a shout and a snap of the reins, he drove the load back on course as if the near catastrophe had never happened.

Paul fell to his knees. Beads of sweat gathered on his forehead, and he was breathing hard, staring at his wrists, hands now buried deep in the mud. Folks around him began picking themselves up and clearing away from the scene.

His mind was somewhere in the place between exhaustion and relief when he was overcome by a wave of warmth spreading from his shoulder through his body. It was accompanied by a heavy weight, and the hairs on his arms stood straight up. Looking to his right, he saw a slender hand resting lightly on his shirt. He followed the arm up to her face. She was looking at him intently, a spark lighting up her soft hazel eyes and strands of sandy hair escaping her untidy bun, her expression serious and filled with worry. Her concern quickly faded into a half smile when his eyes met hers.

"Are you okay?" she asked.

"I...I am." He struggled to find anything to say, even though all of the fight and fatigue from wrestling with the horses and timber-laden sleigh had left his body. He felt completely refreshed, but in some way, he felt smaller with her hand on his shoulder.

"You shouldn't have done that alone. You could've injured yourself. The other men could have helped you," she said.

Paul was taken aback by the blunt critique, and for a moment, all he could do was blink. Finally, he found his voice.

"Looks like I managed just fine. The horses are up and movin', and the haul is on its way. Nobody's hurt." He noticed the defensive tone in his words and felt embarrassed. His cheeks burned.

"Maybe so, but now you're the one stuck in the mud." She gave him a wry smile.

And sure enough, Paul, unbelievably, couldn't seem to free himself from the thick, freezing mud. He tried to push himself up with his hands, but they sunk even deeper as if the ground was pulling him in for a closer look.

Raising an eyebrow, smirk unchanged, she leaned in and said, "Would you like some help?"

He stared blankly back at her. Reaching down, she grabbed a fistful of his soaked shirt and firmly lifted upwards. He rose swiftly to his feet.

All of his words were gone, just like the pines in every forest he'd logged. Paul stared, slack-jawed, at her face. Her sandy hair let off a soft light, making the brisk air seem a little warmer. There was something familiar about this woman, but he couldn't place it. Gathering himself, he chose to save face and be formal with his greeting. "I'm Paul Cunningham, ma'am, and I thank you for your assistance."

There I go again, giving up my last name. What's wrong with me? Paul held his gaze in spite of the urge to look anywhere but in her direction.

"Don't you mean Paul *Bunyan*?" she said. She wore her smile like she was born with it. "Well, Paul, I'm Amelia. Amelia Brennen. It's a pleasure to meet you." And with that, she turned and walked away, stepping confidently through the dimming logging camp, her long overcoat and dress sweeping through the mud like she owned the place. Because, in a way, she did.

———

Amelia Brennen wasn't known to spend much time around her father's business. The near-constant yelling of orders, the whine of the saws in the mill, and the clacking of lumber being stacked made the entire place too chaotic. But the sweet smell of fresh pine sawdust was a comforting scent she'd known since early childhood, and she felt drawn to the mill and logging camps this spring in particular, despite her father's preference that she steer clear due to the rough men and generally unsafe atmosphere.

She had heard of the giant lumberjack who had come to work for her father and was intrigued by the idea of such a living legend. Images of "Jack and the Beanstalk" danced in her mind, but instead of a beanstalk, it was a monstrous evergreen holding a mountain-sized lumberjack in pursuit of Jack and his sickly cow. She had to see the man in person and find out for herself how much of a giant he was.

In their home just blocks away from the Hinckley mill, Amelia sat at the table eating roasted potatoes and salted pork, listening to her parents. Her mother, Alice Brennen, was fair-skinned and blond-haired with faint freckles on the bridge of her nose, a remnant of a sun-loving, carefree childhood long since repressed.

"Alice, I'm sorry, but I have to go again. You know I do. The ice is starting to come out, and we've got too much land to clear. We've got some new men who should be a big help, but I'll need to make sure the crews are on task." Patrick made more eye contact with his plate than with his wife, knowing the winner had already been decided in this battle. He wasn't pleading, he was instructing.

"I know you have to, but the road gets so slick, doesn't it? Can't it wait until things dry up a little more?" Alice, too, knew the decision had been made. Her husband would be leaving, but she had no misgivings in sharing her concern. She looked to Amelia on her left, who was nudging food around her plate. Her daughter also had a way with making herself heard, sometimes a little too loudly, in Alice's opinion. The fact brought Alice just as much frustration as it did pride.

"Father," Amelia interrupted. Both parents looked to their daughter, sensing an impending and dissatisfying request. "I'd like to go with you to the camp, if I may. The house is well taken care of, and I think it would be good for me to better understand how you manage the business." Amelia again imagined the giant lumberjack swaying in the clouds from the top of an impossibly tall pine.

Patrick's brow furrowed, trying to see past the innocent, gentle eyes of his daughter.

"You don't need to concern yourself with your father's business, Amelia." Alice wasn't surprised that her daughter had spoken up but was irritated by her interest in logging and mill work. Amelia always seemed to be reaching for things out of her grasp. Alice felt it again. Pride. Frustration.

"Mother, you are always asking me to care for those around me. I think if I were to see how the camps function, I might have a better understanding of the importance of Father's work."

"You can come along." Patrick spoke without looking at either of the women at the table. Alice glared at her husband, angered by the finality of his words, but she remained quiet. It hadn't gone unnoticed by Patrick Brennen that with no sons and two daughters already married off to men with their own professions, Amelia may be his only heir to the mill. He returned to his food, signaling that the decision was made.

"Really?" Amelia said, startled. She thought her request was going to be denied. She broke into a smile but stifled it equally as fast, not wanting to risk squandering this small victory. "Thank you, Father."

"But you'll stay away from the jacks, you hear? You'll either stick with Jeremiah or stay in the carriage and do your observing through the window."

Alice got up from the table and began collecting the silverware. "Amelia, I'd like you to clean the dishes and make sure to mend your dress this evening. You'll need to stay warm on your upcoming adventure."

Her voice was curt, and the word "adventure" was thrown like a spear in her husband's direction. If she wasn't going to have a say in this decision, then she would at least have a say in who helps with the housework. Alice Brennen picked up her husband's plate as he was about to stab his last slab of ham.

"Oh, I'll take that for you, dear. I don't want you to eat too much before bed. You'll be up all night with stomach pains." Her words were spoken through a smile, but they struck him as if he had fallen into a patch of overgrown nettles.

Patrick carefully handed over his fork, taking a moment to choose his words wisely. The house was still quite cold at night, and sleeping alone made it all the worse. "Good idea," he finally said. "Thank you for dinner, Alice."

And with that, he went over to sit by the fire and enjoy his evening pipe while Amelia hurried off to sew any areas of concern on her dress before the morning's departure.

The next day, Amelia, her father, and Jeremiah set off in a carriage before sunrise to reach camp by midmorning. The carriage bumped along the logging road over roots and ruts for several hours. With the chilled morning air, the carriage windows were shut tight. The only light came from a kerosene lantern sending soft shadows jumping around the small sitting area. Amelia imagined a dense emerald forest outside the windows, but by the time the sun rose and she dared peek through the curtains, she only saw snow, mud, and piles of fractured tree limbs. By the time they arrived, she thought her teeth would fall out from the jostling they'd endured. She stepped out of the carriage and held onto the door while she regained her balance on the unwavering steadiness of the hard ground. Only a few folks milled about the scattered building as the jacks and swampers were already out swinging their axes and rolling their logs.

Mr. Brennen spent several hours reviewing maps with the foreman and Jeremiah, speculating on what could be expected from a winter of steady logging. Amelia attempted to appear interested, but her attention often shifted to the sights around camp. She watched the cook cleaning and packing food to be brought out to the men. He filled large jugs with tea, steam billowing as he poured. Several iron pots filled to the brim with water were boiling with what looked like large black leaves rising and falling in the smoky liquid, and a stale, musty smell wafted from each pot. A slender man, cloaked in the steam, stood nearby and stirred them like a witch hovering over her cauldrons.

"What's he cooking?" Amelia asked Jeremiah, who was standing off to her right.

"Cooking?" Jeremiah asked. He glanced over to the steaming pots and the man prodding them with a wooden paddle. "Well, looks like lice, crab, and bed bug stew to me." Jeremiah laughed at the disgusted look on Amelia's face, satisfied with her reaction.

"I'm only half jokin'," he said. "Those are the spare clothes. They boil 'em every now and then to get the bugs off. Helps everyone sleep a little better if you don't feel all those critters crawling up and down your legs all night. Don't worry. Nobody's gonna drink the water afterward." He laughed again and walked over to Mr. Brennen and the foreman, who were both nibbling on small, dry biscuits. Amelia had lost her appetite, and it likely wouldn't return for a week.

The rest of the day was quiet and uneventful, but slowly, groups of men started to return to camp. She still hadn't seen the giant she imagined would be working the woods when Jeremiah called over to her.

"Amelia, your father is finishing up, so it'll be time to go soon. He asked that I get you into the carriage so we're ready. We'll be getting back after dark as it is."

They began to walk towards the carriage on the south side of camp when they heard the whinnying of horses and yelling voices. Amelia saw the commotion around the sleigh and the horses struggling to stand on the quickly freezing road, then she felt the ground shaking before finally noticing the towering figure with rope in hand running toward the animals. He was startlingly tall, standing an easy foot above everyone else crowded around the sleigh.

Amelia watched as the surrounding horde backed off. The man wrapped the rope around the front of the sled and gathered the reins like Zeus corralling lightning bolts. Then he pivoted and began pulling with the force and effort of Atlas shouldering the world. The massive cargo slowly started sliding and picked up speed as the horses leapt up. The giant collapsed like an old roof under the weight of too much snow. The man had been pulling for less than a minute, but the effort had clearly exasperated his strength and brought him thundering to the ground.

Amelia felt an intense, magnetic connection to this man and was being pulled from her shore to his by a strong riptide. She didn't just see his fatigue, she felt his weakness in her arms and his exhaustion running down her back into her legs. Her heart pounded from the exertion. The skin on her hands burned from the rough rope and tight reins. She suddenly realized that her legs were moving her body toward him under their own accord, and before she could think to stop herself, she was at his side.

Up until now, no matter where her feet fell, Amelia Brennen never felt like she belonged. She had moved across the northern country throughout her childhood along with her two older sisters and younger brother, following her father's dreams of wealth cut from the north. Even when the family settled down in Hinckley, Amelia struggled to find a foothold.

Nearly all she had was handed down from her sisters. Her clothes were worn and showed the stress of years traveled on her sisters' backs. The dresses and stockings had been given to her now that both her sisters were married to successful men in the Hinckley community and had begun good starts on big families. Even the color of her hair was a hand-me-down. But unlike her sisters' hair, who each had the faint tint of copper like their father's, Amelia inherited the same sandy shade of Alice's hair without any trace of flame from her father.

As for her brother, he died in his fourth year from scarlet fever just as they began to settle in Minnesota. Patrick Brennen fled his son's death like wildfire by pouring all of his energy into his business, and Amelia became the son her father no longer had, hence, his lack of objection the day she asked to visit the logging camp. It was his secret hope that she might somehow take to the business. Of course, Patrick Brennen knew all too well that it would be difficult for a woman to be accepted in his position.

Amelia didn't understand it, but after all the wandering through this cold, northern world filled with hardened men, scavenging beasts, and lost indigenous faces, she suddenly felt at home here at the side of this stranger. He was, indeed, a fallen giant, but there was no sign of the menacing, ax-swinging monstrosity she'd imagined.

Reaching out to touch his shoulder, Amelia felt sudden shock and a pulsing heat when her finger first grazed the fabric of his shirt. From the shudder that rippled beneath her hand, she knew he felt it too.

In Love, Summer, 1894

In the evenings I will find you there
By a streamside cold and true
Every strand of sandy hair
Is the shore I'm sailing to

Paul thought of nothing but the kind, smiling face of Amelia Brennen for the next two weeks until his mind became so preoccupied with her that the shanty boys began asking who he was calling to in his sleep.

"Sounds like Bunyan's got a sweetheart hidden somewhere, boys!" The jeering calls and laughter rang around the bunkhouse for the second night in a row.

"Anything you need to tell me, my friend?" Otto grinned a wide, toothy smile beneath his swirling mustache and gave Paul a knowing wink.

"You can just keep your French mouth closed there, Otto," Paul said. He was growing red as a cardinal and leaned in closer to his friend with a look of serious concern. "I didn't say any names last night, did I?"

"No, no. Your sandy-haired secret is safe with me." Otto turned from Paul and shouted to the rest of the bunkhouse. "Time to get to sleep, my friends!"

Come Sunday, when several of the men wanted to head into town to get drunk and play cards, Paul decided to tag along. He strode alongside the wagon carrying the men into Hinckley.

"You comin' for a drink this time?" one of the men on the wagon said. They were all surprised by Paul's presence. It was well known that he never came along when the men were looking to spend what money they had to spare.

"Nah. Need to see 'bout some new clothes. I'm wearin' mine out again. I'll catch up with ya in a bit." Paul casually walked off with a satchel at his side looking for the general store, all the while glancing up and down the streets for anybody he might recognize.

After placing an order for a new pair of wool socks and another pair of canvas slacks, Paul thanked the store manager, ducked out the doorway, and stepped onto Hinckley's Main Street. The day was warm, and most of the men would be liquored up and happy by now, likely singing loudly and off-key in the saloon. The thought made him smile, and he was just reconsidering joining them when he caught sight of a familiar silhouette. The air was stolen from his lungs as he watched Amelia Brennen walk away from him about five houses down and begin to turn off Main Street. Just before she went out of sight, she lifted her gaze and locked onto Paul's slate eyes long enough for him to see a flicker of a smile before she disappeared behind the building.

Paul shook off the shock, bringing himself back to the street as three young boys ran past him chasing a dog. He ran towards the alley, taking a sliding turn through the mud to face an empty street lined with wooden buildings and a few broken crates towering on his left. She was nowhere to be seen. Paul took a few steps forward and just about tripped as he heard fabric tear at his feet. Looking down, he saw the cuffs of his pants dragging at his heels. His left pant leg had caught on an iron rod which had surfaced through the mud like a rising fish.

"You sure get yourself into trouble often, don't you?" a familiar voice said from behind him.

Paul swung around, staggering free from the metal thorn that had snagged his clothes. Amelia Brennen was standing in the middle of the alley, one brow cocked upwards, eyes twinkling, a charcoal wool overcoat buttoned snugly up to her chin. Paul straightened up and smiled.

"For some reason, I thought you were taller the last time I saw you," Amelia said. She sized up the man whose clothing seemed baggy around his wrists and ankles.

The two stared at each other for a long moment. A dog barked from the street behind them, interrupting the silence they were savoring like a last meal. Apparently, the children had caught up to the canine.

"It's nice to see you too, Miss Brennen." Paul took a step towards Amelia. He stood as tall as he could in an attempt at saving face. "If you're willin', the boys aren't headin' back to camp for another hour or so, and we could take a walk if ya like? That is, if you'd do me the honor."

"Oh, come now. You don't need to be formal with me, Paul Cunningham. Amelia is fine, and of course I'd like to take a walk with you. I've been hoping you'd be coming out of the pines since we met."

It went against everything Alice Brennen had taught Amelia. Being forward in the company of a strange man, let alone a lumberjack, would have sent her mother to her grave, but Amelia felt comfortable standing in front of Paul. And now, walking next to him on the familiar streets of Hinckley instead of the logging roads of the wild pineries, he didn't seem outlandishly tall by any means, at least not as tall as she remembered.

"So, where did you spend your childhood, Mr. Cunningham?" Amelia figured Paul didn't talk to many women and felt the need to drive the conversation. She playfully emphasized the "Mr." to try and ease the tension that was clearly coursing through his veins.

"Maine, mostly. But been movin' westward ever since I left home."

"Why is that?"

"Not sure really. Guess I've just felt pulled in this direction. That, and once I've taken down the biggest trees, I just need to move along and find the next ones. I can log in a day more than most men can log in a week, you know? So it's either that, or I guess I just get annoyed of young jacks coming to take a look at Big Paul Bunyan."

He described the two blond-haired boys in Wisconsin who had danced around him like puppies, and Amelia laughed at the thought of the Norwegians who had come to lay eyes on the great logging giant of the north. She could empathize with their curiosity. Paul couldn't help but chuckle along with her contagious laughter.

"How 'bout you? Have you been movin' 'round, or are ya native to these parts?"

Amelia halted. Paul stopped and turned to face her. "You know, none of us are native, Paul. There were people here long before us. We've just pushed them out of sight. But, to answer your question, I suppose I have a similar story, but we've been in Hinckley for a lot of years now. Long enough that it feels like home, anyway. Whatever that means. The way Father's mill is doing, I don't expect us to be moving on anytime soon. The town is fine enough, but someday I'd like to move on and explore."

The pair strolled through the side streets and alleys of Hinckley. Paul told her of the logging camps in Maine, Michigan, and Wisconsin, leaving out the details of his parents. As they walked, the back of his hand grazed Amelia's knuckles, and a buzzing sensation ran through his body. He felt charged, the way the air feels beneath a gigantic thunderhead just before the first lightning strike. The sensation sobered him up.

"You know your father would fire me on the spot if he saw me walking alone with you."

"Well, I think that depends," Amelia said.

"What do ya mean, 'depends'?"

"I mean that his opinion on whether or not to keep you employed likely depends on your intentions for walking by my side. If you mean to disrespect me, then yes, he'll likely have you beaten and left for the wolves."

Paul laughed. "And if I have nothin' but the highest respect for ya?"

"I think he would let me make my own decision, and you'd still have a job, for now. But I think we both know your respect for me could be better, given the fact that we've been hiding in alleys for the better part of the last hour." She smiled as Paul blushed. He watched the peach-colored sky dance off her sandy hair, then his blushing turned to a frown, suddenly realizing that the sun was setting and their time was about up. "The boys will be heading back by now." Paul looked to Amelia with regret written in the lines of his face. "I'm sorry, miss. I mean, Amelia. But I need to get goin'."

Amelia reached out and grabbed Paul's hand. She felt the rough palm, like a poorly tanned hide, and wondered how many trees it had cut down since it began swinging an ax.

"Will you come to visit Hinckley again?" Her eyes never strayed from his. Paul couldn't look away even if he wanted to. He felt pulled towards her, and she glowed like an ember deep within a hearth.

"I would really like that. But, I don't think your father'd appreciate me spending time around ya. So maybe, for now, it's probably best if we don't share with too many folks that we're meeting, if ya know what I mean. I'd hate for you to get in trouble."

"Me? Get in trouble?" she said. They both laughed, knowing her punishment would weigh much less than his. "Have it your way, Paul Cunningham. Would you like to meet again as the weather warms? Maybe you'd prefer an evening stroll?"

She was still holding his hand, but now he took both of hers in return and looked at them inquisitively as if not quite sure what his next step would be. He felt like he was beginning a journey without knowing the destination.

Amelia's hands were light as butterfly wings, but they felt steady as the ground beneath his feet. Paul bent down and softly kissed the back of her hand. She felt the tickle of the rough hairs of his mustache and beard as they scraped her skin, and her cheeks turned as red as the sunset. Paul's burned like the falling sun.

"That sounds perfect. I'll be back next Sunday around sunset. I'll wait for you at the depot," he said.

Paul gave her hands a squeeze, then let them go, jogging off in the opposite direction in search of the drunken party that would be making the long journey back to camp.

The entire ride back, by the light of their lanterns, the lumberjacks sang songs about long-lost love and told tall tales of forbidden maidens. Paul listened quietly but was unable to suppress his grin, knowing he was likely the only person on the drunken wagon who could tell a tale of forbidden love and not have to worry about being called a liar. But, of course, he kept his story to himself.

———

Think of every love story or legend told where an inexplicable force fiercely binds two star-crossed lovers. The love burns white-hot and can't be left alone for more than a few hours without creating an unstable nuclear cascade tumbling toward implosion. Stolen glances. Rocks thrown at moonlit windows. Flirtatious hands reaching out on busy streets. It is an addiction without reason, and it ambushes the two players with its intensity. This is the best way to describe the connection between Paul and Amelia. Irrational. Magnetic. Wonderful.

Paul continued to work as hard as he could by day, but his long days were followed by silent escapes from the camp at night and moonlit walks through the streets of Hinckley. Meeting at night was the best way for the two to avoid drawing attention to their budding relationship. Whenever he was with her, Amelia thought that Paul didn't seem as tall. She could almost look him directly in the eyes on the darkest nights.

"Where do you walk off to when you go on your evening strolls, Bunyan?" the camp cook asked as Paul started walking away from the bunkhouse. The cook, like many others, had noticed that shortly after dinner, Paul would sharpen his ax, then head off away from camp. He was never there when the lamps went out, but he was always in his bed come morning. It had gone on like this for weeks.

"Nowhere in particular," Paul said. "There's just something about the forest at night, I guess. Helps me relax."

"Just don't let your work suffer, or Mr. Brennen'll hear 'bout it and you'll be looking for a new forest to wander." The cook turned, spat on the ground, and rubbed the splatter into the dirt with the toe of his boot.

Once Paul was out of sight of camp, he picked up speed and flew through the woods like an American kestrel, dodging piles of slash and leaping over creek beds. He could cover the trip in less than half an hour and barely break a sweat.

Once he made it to town, Paul would sit with his back against the wall of the train depot, beneath the cover of a tall maple tree with leaves that rustled like pages of the Bible. There he would wait until the sun fully set and twilight's last glow bowed to the moon and stars. When all was dark, footsteps in the loose gravel would start to make their way down the street from west of the station. Amelia typically found Paul sitting beneath the maple, humming a logging song to the squeaking bats fluttering above.

The two met like this several nights a week, walking the streets of Hinckley.

"Don't you get tired when you get back so late?" Amelia tried to stifle a yawn as Ursa Major scooped up a shooting star above their heads.

"Nah. I really don't need that much sleep most nights. Sometimes it catches up with me, but when the boys and I are really into an acreage and clearing land like a tornado, I swear I could barely sleep at all. Or eat or drink for that matter. It's a little strange, and I've never told anyone, but I can go for a week or so with just a few sips of water and maybe a small something to nibble on."

"Really? That's amazing," Amelia said.

"I guess so. Can't explain it. Just always been that way," Paul replied. He was relieved that she believed him and didn't seem frightened by his confession.

Amelia let out a sigh. "I'd waste away in an afternoon if I didn't eat or drink." A shudder traveled down her back as she thought of the hunger, and her stomach gave a small growl as if to protest the idea of a fast. They laughed.

"Well, I can't have that, now can I? I better start bringing you something to snack on just to be safe," Paul said.

Amelia smiled. "You might have to if these walks keep getting longer like they seem to."

"How 'bout meeting during the daytime? Next Sunday is an off-day. If the weather's good, I'd expect we could meet northeast of town by the river. There's a nice clearing by a little aspen grove. Wouldn't be more than an hour's walk for you, forty-five minutes if you're really movin'." There was just enough moonlight that Paul was able to trace a map in the dirt with his finger. "You think you can find it?"

"You're not the only one who walks in the woods, you know. Don't be silly, of course I'll find it." Amelia turned to walk back in the direction of her home, then stopped and looked back at Paul. "Is there anything I can bring you next week? I could sneak one of my mother's biscuits and some cured ham."

"No, no. You just show up. I'll bring some of the finest loggin' camp food you've ever seen. I'll take care of all of it," Paul assured her.

Amelia gave him an amused, yet uncertain look. "Well, sounds like this will be quite the adventure after all. If the food is anything like I've heard, I'll be walking out of those woods wearing plaid and growing a beard."

Paul let out a loud, deep laugh. "Now that would be something!"

The west winds were kind over the next few days, and the following Sunday was a day when most of the shanty men would take the day to sharpen their axes, enjoy a day of drinking, and rest. For Amelia and Paul, it was the perfect day to spend beneath the flickering shade of the young aspen trees. The spade-shaped leaves were fresh out of their buds, but they still managed to flip back and forth in the breeze, projecting an ever-changing pattern of light on the ground where the couple lay.

"So, what's so wrong with a lumberjack anyway? Don't you think your father would warm up to me?" Paul was lying on his back, looking up to the sky, hands folded beneath his head. He turned to Amelia sitting next to him. Her hair was down, and a few strands caught the air currents, shining like thin, floating strands of gold.

"I told you," Amelia said, "he always said to stay away from lumberjacks. He wanted us girls to marry bankers or businessmen. He says there is security in that type of man. So far, he's succeeded with two out of three. You'd think that would be good enough."

"Security, eh? I don't know about that. I mean, that man'll be spending days indoors and nights countin' pennies. If that's what security means, then you can keep it. I'm perfectly happy out here in the wind." Paul brought his hands to his side and rested his head down on the mossy floor next to Amelia.

The picnic he had packed sat on a large stump, now serving as a table. Paul brought a jug of tea and a pile of biscuits. Amelia brought cheese from her parents' cellar.

"Well, how do you plan to take care of me, Mr. Lumberjack?" Amelia had enjoyed poking fun at the man she was getting to know. For as confident as he seemed to be, he really was easy to crack.

"Hmm." He rolled onto an elbow, looking into her gleaming eyes, flecks of gold and green among the soft browns of her irises. They were eyes that gave the impression they held more knowledge than all the books one could read. "I figure that by the end of summer, I'll be able to save enough money to buy a small property somewhere up north. Maybe forty acres of cutaway land. I walked through a young town named Ely last winter. It's pretty country up there, ya know."

"How far is it? Think we could make it before they know we're gone?" She was smiling as she looked up at the clean, clear, blue sky.

Paul knew she was joking but sensed a drop of sincerity in the question. "It's a good hundred miles or so from here. I'll need money for some horses and provisions first, but that won't take me long. I'm paid more than most other men," he said.

"You know…we could ask my father for some help…and his blessing. It's okay to ask for help." Seeing his defensive glance, Amelia continued, "He really might give us some money to get started. That is, assuming you'll be asking me to marry you first," she added with a grin.

Paul coughed out a burst of laughter. "Well, I'll be. I never thought I'd be the one getting proposed to! Miss Amelia Brennen, you've just made me the happiest man on God's Great Earth." Paul let out more laughter, but then came to a stop, and his tone turned serious. "Listen, I do want to marry you. But I don't want to ask for your father's money or help. What kind of man would I be if the first thing I did after asking for his blessing to take his daughter away was to ask him for the money to do so? I can't do that, Amelia. I need to make this money on my own. If I don't, I'll owe your father for the rest of our lives."

"If he is giving you my hand, won't you owe him anyway?" she said. Her quick wit was always as direct as a well-thrown hatchet.

"You always have the right thing to say, don't you?" Paul said smiling, but still serious. "It's true, though. Your father is a stubborn man, and you're his last little girl. I've gotta do right by you."

A soft wind picked up and rustled the leaves above them. They teeter-tottered on their slender stems, and Amelia inched herself into Paul's warmth.

She looked up at the saplings. "My father once told me that they rarely used to see these this far up north. They move in after we clear the big pines. Closing in on us. The white-tailed deer too. He said that those used to live further south and it's a shame they've come north because they carry disease that makes the other animals sick too." They sat quietly, synchronizing their breathing. "What do you think it would look like if we didn't clear these forests?"

Paul wasn't really listening to her words so much as the sound of them. "Oh, we'd have trees higher than you can see and twice as wide as a wagon. And it would be the perfect place to start chopping. I had a foreman once tell me that the worst type of tree is the one that stands. As far as I'm concerned, he just might be right." He turned to look at her. The sun highlighted the lighter blonde strands in her hair. "Your hair is one of the most beautiful things I've ever seen."

"Well thank you, but, Paul, I'm serious. What if we didn't log with such a...well, what if we were more careful about it? Doesn't it seem strange to you to totally change a place without a thought for what could happen?"

She had his attention now. "What do you mean, 'what could happen'?"

"Well, the aspens. The deer. The Native Americans that lived here. There must be some sort of payment to be made for...the way we treat the land and its people. I just feel like there is another way to get what we all want." Amelia didn't have the answer she was looking for. She was hoping to connect with Paul on this line of thinking so they could find it together, but one glance told her that she was losing him. It didn't seem like he saw her concern.

Paul's brow relaxed from the deep furrow, and he put on a boyish grin. "I think I could listen to you talk forever," he said, reaching for Amelia to pull her close.

"Well, we can't stay forever because we are far from home and the sun is starting to drop. We really better get going."

Amelia rocked up to her knees and kissed Paul. He savored the sweet, grassy flavor of tea on her lips. She stood up, laughing at his stunned face, and ran off towards the horses that were munching on nearby shrubbery. He shook the dizzy feeling from his head and leapt to his feet, catching up to her in a few strides. He tapped her lightly on her right shoulder as he ran around her left, sending her spinning in pursuit, both giggling like the children they were.

"Amelia, hang on a minute." Paul caught her by the shoulders, his smile gone. He looked at his feet, shifting uncomfortably, but finally lifted his chin to catch her eyes. She seemed taller. They were almost face-to-face. "I...I have something I want you to have, if you'd take it, that is."

From the pocket along his right thigh, Paul raised a tarnished, golden chain from which an oval pendant swung in the starlight. Amelia lifted the necklace and squinted in the dim light to see the winding design laced around the clasp. She unhinged the clasp and opened the pendant like a river mussel. Inside, she found a familiar set of innocent eyes trying their best to bottle up a smile.

"My mother gave me this picture when I left home, and I found someone to put it in this necklace. I'd like you to have it if ya would," Paul said.

Amelia gently closed the locket and swung the necklace over her head, lifting her hair to let the chain rest against her skin. The metal oval lay in the small depression where her collarbones met.

"Come on, Mr. Lumberjack, it's getting late." She grabbed his hand, and they ran through the twilight, laughing like loons and dodging shadows.

———

July in northern Minnesota is a special time of year. The days are long. The sun rises around 5:30 am and sets shortly after 8:00 pm, and the soft light of dusk stays for almost another hour before darkness truly sets in. Once the sun drops below the horizon, the temperature cools and the mosquitoes rush from the cover of greenery to find the closest uncovered patch of skin. They dash like the madmen of the Oklahoma land rush, seeking real estate that will be fruitful and, with any luck, safe enough to allow a quick escape, belly full of blood, before a swatting hand ends their one-track-mind life.

If you are lucky enough to have either the type of skin that is impervious to the little bloodsuckers, or you merely have that unknown deterrent which keeps mosquitoes uninterested, the northern July magic-hour starting just before sunset is the perfect time to find a quiet corner of solitude, lie down, and drift into a sea of calm reflection and peace.

As for Paul, his skin was more than thick enough. The mosquitoes would always quickly give up and move on to other, softer-skinned prey. One day, after he had finished a long day of work followed by dinner with the other choppers and swampers and Amelia was back in Hinckley helping with a new nephew, he took the opportunity to lie down on the edge of camp and let his mind wander.

Amelia's smiles came to him just as quickly as she had entered his life. He had tried not to think of his mother since her death, but Paul thought she would have liked Amelia. The previous week, he had gotten a letter finalizing the sale of his parents' possessions, minus fees and services, of course. The money had been placed in a bank near their home, and Paul could pick it up at his leisure. The family ox, which had been quite old, passed away under the care of a local farmer.

Paul was sad to hear that his old ox was gone. He loved that strong-shouldered animal. Its hair was matted and silvery like a cloudy day but always warm to the touch. He had almost returned home just for the animal but decided to stay up north. *Would I have gone back if I hadn't met Amelia?* he thought.

The wind changed with his train of thought. He listened to the bubbling of the nearby creek and looked at his hands. His calluses were smooth like the stones peeking through the shallows of the stream, clearly visible in the low water level from the summer's drought.

Paul thought of the tall pines he'd cut over the years and the satisfaction of each final swing of his ax followed by the slowly accelerating descent of the timber. When a large tree completes its arc and hits the ground, it sends a shockwave through a man's chest. It was the most wonderful feeling he'd known until he met Amelia. She doubled that shockwave, and then some.

I'm sure I can make enough money by fall, he thought. *I'll talk to her father as soon as I have enough. Once we're married, we'll head north.*

He planned to start his own small farm, or perhaps a lumber company. He was capable enough to do it himself, at least get it started anyway. All he needed was a good set of horses and, eventually, the equipment to start his own mill.

Another breeze stirred the leaves nearby, this one carrying a crisp preview of fall and the sweet smell of the earliest falling leaves. Soon that scent would saturate the air like lilacs in spring. Somewhere nearby, a small animal shifted in the waning moments of daylight.

His eyelids grew heavy, and the lingering warmth of the day wrapped around him like a blanket. After a hefty yawn, his eyes began to water and he blinked slowly, giving into the comfort of the quickly approaching peaceful evening.

A loud rustle disturbed the nearby leaves. Paul looked up to see a rabbit jumping through the underbrush into the clearing by his feet. It looked directly at Paul and continued hopping toward him. As the rabbit got closer, it started to grow. Paul blinked a few times to be sure he was seeing things correctly. The rabbit was stretching, its ears folding back and turning black just as the fur on its head turned black and grew into long, sleek, shining hair. The rabbit's face changed to the face of a dark-eyed man, and the fur-covered body transformed into the tan skin of a man wearing an animal hide around his waist. His hair was twisted into a braid and rested on his muscular shoulder. Paul sat up straight and tried to push himself to his feet, but his legs wouldn't budge. He could hardly comprehend the scene unfolding before him as the man began walking forward, hands held out and eyes looking to the empty sky, speaking words Paul couldn't understand. Small pine trees sprouted where his feet fell. He stopped and turned his gaze to Paul, who was stuck to the ground in shock. Paul looked deep into the eyes of the man and felt himself being pulled through the obsidian orbs, as if he were being washed away and thrown over a waterfall into darkness. Once the black around him became completely thick, the visions began.

Paul's parents were in front of him, holding hands and calling his name. They didn't look frightened, but he felt the concern coming from his mother's eyes. From their feet, sparks and embers spun up like a cyclone and washed Samantha and Andrew Cunningham away from this vision. The fiery storm grew steadily and began reaching for him with its leaping arms. The last thing he saw before the man reached down and grabbed his shoulders to shake him awake was Amelia shrouded in the tornado of flames, calling out to Paul for help.

The Blessing, August 1894

If you take a bowl in your hand and set it firmly on a table,
the sound produced will expose the integrity of the ceramic.
A sturdy bowl without any cracks will make a noise like a confident knock at your door.
A bowl split with hairline fractures will sound weak as a rotten floorboard.
The vessel may still hold water, and most definitely fruit or grains,
but leave it for a time filled with liquid,
and slowly the cracks will show
as the bowl begins to drain.
Sealing the cracks early will stave off irritation
from stained wooden tables and wasted broth.
At some point, the cracks spread like cobwebs
and the bowl becomes brittle, flakes chipping off.
For the stubborn person unwilling to intervene,
they will end up with a shattered bowl and wet floor,
fruitlessly hoping to find enough pitch to piece everything back together,
all the while thirsty for a drink, wishing they had more.

Patrick Liam Brennen had left Ireland as a child with his parents and eight siblings in search of opportunity. America was a shining star across the ocean with free land and a chance to climb a ladder that didn't exist in County Kilkenny, where the Brennen family had lived for generations. As the youngest of the lot, Patrick had to fight for every scrap of food and attention he could find. Nothing came easily for his family, and he learned shortly after setting foot in the dense northern forests of New Hampshire that a better life was only going to come to those determined enough to seize it. He may have been the youngest Brennen, but he was by far the smartest and most driven.

As a young teen, he had convinced his siblings to start their own logging operation by helping farmers clear fields and selling wood to the local mills. His parents bought into the project and provided the early capital needed to get off the ground. They started small and continued the push westward, and over time, the company grew beyond the Brennen siblings.

The cunning mind of Patrick Brennen had translated into dependable, quality results. This, in turn, meant loyal customers, investors, and good money. In the early logging years, Patrick Brennen married Alice, the daughter of a banker, and they began their family as they left New Hampshire for northern Michigan. When he heard the rumors of the great white pines of Wisconsin and Minnesota, he found his way to Hinckley and proceeded to build one of the finest lumber mills in the region. The fact that he didn't have a living son to pass the business off to weighed heavily on his mind, and, so far, his two sons-in-law were unlikely to be part of the family business. However, there was still an off-chance with Amelia if she ever settled down. Thus far, there had yet to be a suitor he would trust with the mill, let alone with his daughter.

It also wasn't lost on him that Amelia might have enough fire in her to run the business herself, but a woman running a lumber mill was unheard of as far as he was concerned. However, if any woman could do it, she could.

When word had come that Paul Bunyan was in town looking for

work, Patrick said a little prayer that the giant logger might find his way to his doorstep. If even half of what people said about the big fella were true, he'd be an excellent asset to the company. If Paul came to Brennen Lumber Mill, Patrick would try to pay him the regular wage with the temptation of a raise, which would still get Patrick more than his money's worth. He only hoped that this logging giant didn't bring along any of the baggage that often follows unique characters who float through the frontier. As it usually does, time would tell. The thought of Paul becoming a possible solution for the future of the mill never even came close to entering Patrick Brennen's mind.

———

August was nearly over, and Paul was working twice as hard as the other men. Whispers had started around the camp that one of Mr. Brennen's employees was sneaking around with one of his daughters, and based on Mr. Brennen's attitude of late, it was safe to assume that he had heard the rumors as well. And given that two of the three daughters were already spoken for, the math on the daughter in question was pretty easy.

Paul was back at the mill in Hinckley to help resupply the camp and was taking a moment to grind the blades of his ax and give them a quick oil. He always preferred to do this job himself since the blacksmith's standards at camp for what was considered sharp were apparently akin to a soup spoon.

Paul eyed up one of the blades of his ax, peering down the profile of the razor-sharp edge that seemed to disappear into the taper. He was just about to test the blade by shaving a few hairs off the side of his wrist when one of the mill managers approached with a message. Mr. Brennen wanted to have a word with him in his office. Paul nodded politely and followed, grabbing a blackened, oily rag and carefully running it over the warm edges of the double-bit head of his ax. Paul's expression was nonchalant, but his heart was pounding like a herd of buffalo thundering inside his chest.

As he walked, Paul could hear the fabric of his pants scraping along the dirt floor. They were cuffed at the ankles and swayed loosely around his legs.

"You slimming down there, Bunyan? Feeling alright?" Otto had asked the previous week, noticing the sag in Paul's clothes.

"If I am, it's only from me out-logging ya every day. Ya must be getting old, Otto. I've been almost tripling your count each week." The taunt deflected the attention off Paul's loss in height every time. Still, it hadn't gone unnoticed by Paul that over the last several months, his monolithic size had been ebbing like a receding flood.

Most of his clothes seemed too long for him now. Uncuffed, his shirtsleeves and pant legs inched over his fingertips and toes, and he relied on his suspenders more than ever these days. Since he was born, he had always gotten taller, but every time he was with Amelia, he felt his body giving in to the weight of his love for her. He couldn't quite describe the sensation. He didn't feel a loss of strength, but instead, each time they met was like returning home after a long absence. With every deep exhale in her presence, he seemed to give up a small amount of height, as if she were bringing him back down from the tops of the trees. Paul liked that the two seemed to fit together more and more. With each inch lost, he moved a mile closer to her heart.

Entering the dark office building, Paul noticed the dusty rays of sunshine projecting through the few windows and cracks in the wood-paneled walls. He thought of Amelia and the way she had described the stars on a recent night together. They had been lying on their backs, staring at the endless starry haze of the Milky Way.

"The stars aren't that miraculous, you know." She could shatter the most silent moments with beautiful simplicity. Her words pulled Paul back from the night sky he was floating in.

"Oh really? They seem pretty miraculous to me."

"How so?" she asked.

"I don't know. Those tiny lights fill up the night sky, and every once in a while, one shoots across it like a fleeing rabbit. And then they leave that tail just long enough for you to reassure yourself ya saw it. Seems pretty amazing to me," said Paul.

"Well, yes, that is pretty amazing, but I guess what I'm saying is it's not the stars in the sky that are the amazing part. It's the space between the stars that's really amazing. If the stars are out there shining and floating in that sky, what's left in the darkness all around them?"

Paul pondered this for a moment, finally giving up as he came up empty. "I think, maybe, that's something only God knows, Amelia."

"Well, when I meet Him, I'm gonna ask," she said.

Paul let out a short laugh. "Be sure to let me know what He says."

Amelia looked over at Paul. She loved the way his eyes betrayed his masculinity. They were the eyes of a child. The eyes of a boy who believed in a limitless world. They were gentle and whimsical, not the weather-worn eyes of so many men she'd been courted by, men who had been hammered down to fit the world around them. With Paul, she saw a partner who grew against the grain the same way she did. She didn't like how tightly he held onto his logging, but everyone needs a purpose, and she understood that.

They kissed in the night and lay quietly for a few more moments. In the distance, an owl called out, letting others know she was hunting.

Amelia figured the bird would be staking a claim on her hunting grounds for the upcoming change in seasons.

Amelia never could decide what season was her favorite. Each one seemed necessary to fully appreciate the benefits of the others.

"What do you like more? Fall or winter?" she asked.

The distant gaze accompanied by his contented expression made Paul look like a person enjoying a fond memory as he turned over his answer.

"Well, most people would tend to say fall, I suppose, cause of the pretty colors and all. Maybe summer with the warmth and sun. But I don't know. When the snow falls and the air feels clean and crisp in my chest and the sounds of the forest are muffled, I feel strong in a way that is hard to explain. I feel like I'm part of the north just as much as the wolves and big cats."

"Me too," Amelia replied. "I think it's an important part of life. The winter months give us time to reflect and to be reborn in the springtime. I feel many people don't see it that way, but without winter, it would be hard to come into spring rejuvenated and ready to start something new."

Paul felt her turn to look at him. With the moon nowhere to be seen, he had to strain to see the striking features of her face as she spoke again.

"When do you think we'll start our life, Paul?" she asked. "When do you think we will be reborn and move out of this place?"

"Pretty soon, I think," said Paul. "I've got a fair bit saved up, and I think with one more winter, and maybe a spring drive, we'll have enough. And I know what you're gonna say..." Paul cut in as he sensed Amelia starting to interject. "I know we could ask your father for money, but, Amelia, it's like I told ya. If I can't make the money myself, how can I take care of ya? I'll never be good enough for ya, in his eyes anyway.

Once I have the money, I'll ask him for your hand." Paul pulled Amelia close, and the two sunk into the starry night.

Now, back in the mill, as Paul placed his hand on Mr. Brennen's office door, it seemed he may be having that conversation with Amelia's father sooner than he thought.

———

Mr. Brennen was at his desk, sifting through a large pile of papers. He glanced up over his spectacles as Paul walked in.

"Oh, thank you for coming in. Have a seat, Cunningham," he said.

Mr. Brennen was the only person there, besides Amelia, who seemed to remember the lumberjack's true name. Paul sat, the wooden chair creaking beneath his weight, and quietly listened to Mr. Brennen's pen scratch across his ledger.

"Paul, I've got a few cruisers scouting up north, and there's some land available for us to start logging. Big pines. Wide as you are tall, or so I'm told. Old trees, anyway. I'd like to get the deal settled by mid-September or so and start moving up that way to get clearing. With the right team, we should be able to fill up the rivers in time for ice-out next spring. You're the strongest man in my outfit. You've got a good head on your shoulders. I'd like you to lead it."

Almost automatically, Paul answered, "Yes, sir."

He thought of how this fit into his plans with Amelia. The timing was right, and she'd run away with him today if he agreed to it, but he could feel his ax swinging into those tall pines, pulling him in rhythmically. How he longed to be on at least one last big drive through the colossal trees of the north. It would be hard to be further away from Amelia, but this could work in his favor. With a productive winter and spring, he'd have more than enough to get started on his own and support Amelia along the way. In the end, this might be the best way to get close to her for good.

"Thank you, sir." Paul paused, then cautiously continued, "You know, I had considered taking some time off at some point, sir. Just for a little while. Thinking of starting a family, you know?" he added hastily, giving a searching eye toward the top of Mr. Brennen's head, which was buried in his work. Mr. Brennen's pen paused at this, the pointed tip hovering above his ledger. He began writing again.

"Hmm...well, there'll be plenty of time for that after this last haul. Knowing you, you'll move through this forest in no time. By next summer, you'll be free to do as you please." He continued to scribble in the crosshatch of rows and columns that covered the sheet of paper.

"Yes, sir. Absolutely. Will that be all, sir?"

"Yes, just start talking to the boys and get to pickin' your team. Get a good crew together, and you'll get that time off before you know it," Mr. Brennen said. "Oh, I know Ola Värmlänning is still around town looking for work, but that drunk needs to head back south where he came from, so make sure he doesn't find his way onto your team."

"Yes, sir. I'll do that." Paul grinned. He had heard several stories of the clumsy American Swede named Ola and was happy to steer clear of careless men like that. Paul was just about to step out the door when Mr. Brennen called back.

"And Cunningham, Amelia is a good girl. She's honest and strong. True to herself. I won't give my blessing to any man who doesn't see and respect that." Mr. Brennen held Paul's gaze, letting the words sink in. A tree could have crashed through the roof of his office and it wouldn't have broken the stare. A silent agreement was made. Paul would have to do this work to earn the blessing, and if he hurt Amelia, he would likely end up dead. He nodded to Mr. Brennen and walked into the mill yard.

Deep down, he was thankful for the conversation. Not because the secret of his relationship with Amelia was finally free, but because he now had a solid excuse to do one more hard season of logging. The blessing was contingent upon it. It was an excuse to do the only thing he loved nearly as much as Amelia, and guiltily, at times he loved it possibly more. If he had to choose between the two, of course he'd pick her, but the thought of having her at his side and being able to bring down a few more giants with his bare hands was just about as perfect a world as he could imagine.

September 1, 1894

It only takes a day
It only takes a moment
Everything can change in the fraction of a second
Every falling leaf
Every fallen tree
Any of these could be
What takes you from me

Paul had one last week of sending logs down the river before he had to get ready to start up the new camp for Mr. Brennen. He was back in Hinckley for an afternoon and decided to visit Amelia at her house. Alice slowly opened the door at his knock. Her jaw tensed when she saw his face. She gave him the slightest of nods and called for Amelia.

Amelia came to the door, and when she saw Paul, she gave a quiet gasp, nervously glancing between her mother and the lumberjack. "What are you doing here?"

Paul faced Alice. "Hello, ma'am. May I have a word with your daughter?"

"You may." Alice could see honesty and a good heart in this tall boy, and she knew her daughter saw it too. She wasn't surprised when Patrick had told her the news about Amelia and Paul. "I'll be right inside, Amelia, if you need me." She shut the door and left the two on the porch of the house.

"My parents know about us?" Amelia whispered frantically. She felt exposed and vulnerable, like an owl whose tree had vanished into thin air. "How long have you known?"

"Since last week," Paul said. "Your father called me into his office to talk about work. That's when he told me. Didn't seem too mad though," he added. Amelia's eyes grew so wide that he could walk right through them.

"What happened? What did you say?" Her mind raced and was just grabbing hold of the possibility that maybe, just maybe, the two might be able to leave before winter. Her heart was beating like a hummingbird's wings.

"Well, he wants me to work through the spring. There's a new plot of land with more board feet than he can handle. He needs me to lead his crew and clear it up. It'll be good money, and if we get through it, he says he'll give us his blessing." Paul saved this detail for the end, expecting Amelia to jump up and kiss him with overwhelming joy. Instead, she stood, stiff as a board, eyes beginning to narrow.

"He said what?" she asked.

"Your father said he'd give us his blessing. I just have to work through the spring. It's great, right?" Paul sensed a storm brewing in the body standing before him. The muscles along Amelia's jawline rippled as she clenched her teeth, and the air between them charged with electricity.

"This is absurd! If he knows about us and is withholding his blessing for his own benefit, we should just leave without it. Let's take the money we have and just start our new life right now. We'll be fine." She was half pleading and half growling at him as she paced back and forth.

"Well, I gotta do the work, Amelia. Why are you so upset? I figured you'd be pleased," Paul said.

"I honestly can't believe it. The both of you are just so stubborn and selfish. I expect him to put his business first, so that's no surprise, but it doesn't sound like you put up much of a fight, Paul. All that strength and you can't even see when someone's taking advantage of you."

Paul suppressed a brief defensive impulse and pushed through his guilt, holding firm to his decision to work through spring. "The money will be a great help, and we would regret not having your father's formal blessing. Ya know we would."

This is true, Amelia thought, but she still couldn't let it go. "Paul, I love you. I want to be with you. I know you love your ax and conquering the woods and all, but I need you to love me more than your strength." Exasperated, she shouted, "You can't chop all the trees! There will always be another tree to cut down, but I won't let you keep choosing them over me."

"I won't," he pleaded. "Listen, he's not pullin' a sheet over my eyes. I want to be in his favor, and if I don't do this, then we might as well both be fatherless." An image of Andrew Cunningham flashed before Paul's eyes, but he blinked it away.

Amelia studied Paul's face, and he could tell that she knew where his mind had traveled. She bit her lower lip and nodded, her eyes red with passion.

Paul continued, "I'm gonna head up north with a few boys this week to get the camp ready, and then I'll be back for a day or so before the entire team heads up to get started. We'll talk about it more in a few days, okay?" He could see that she was still upset. Small fires burned on her cheekbones. *She sure is a stubborn thing, isn't she,* he thought fondly. "Amelia, it's just till spring. Then we'll have your father's blessing and our entire lives together."

She looked down at the small, brass-colored locket she wore around her neck, holding a picture of the man she loved, and wrapped her fingers around it like a precious stone. Then, Amelia looked up at Paul, reached forward, and tugged on his plaid-covered chest, bringing him close. She kissed him hard with a mixture of love and anger. Amelia pulled away and looked deep into his pewter eyes, the color of a winter storm.

Today, hers were as dark and rich as soil, filled with wisdom, a place where roots grow deep and strong. Amelia was letting him go, but Paul couldn't quite tell if she believed things would work out the way he thought.

Amelia inched back, releasing him. She surprised him with a soft, knowing smile out of the corner of her mouth and started walking backward, her smiling gaze stuck on Paul. In a sudden, graceful movement, she turned on her heel and walked off the porch and away from the house, her shoulder blades shifting like the waves of Lake Superior in her earthy dress, the colors a mixture of his mother's chestnut eyes and the rusted iron ore of the Great North.

———

A selection of Mr. Brennen's logging crew, along with Paul, made its way north to the newly claimed woodland. The journey took longer than Paul thought, lasting a full two-and-a-half days, but it was worth it. The forest was virgin in a way only wilderness can be. Only the feet of wild animals and generations of Native Americans had called this land home, as far as Paul knew. Now it was all his to conquer. Paul wanted to move as quickly as possible getting the men set up for camp before he returned to Hinckley to finalize details for the fall and winter.

"Let's get this road cleared and start building up walls for the bunkhouse, boys," he said.

A slender man with hollow eyes and sickly skin was helping saw logs to size for the sleeping quarters. "You think we're gonna be able to clear all this up by springtime? Sure seems like a lot," he said.

"We don't have a choice," Paul replied to the man, who looked far too ill to be up there. This jack wasn't his first choice, but the pickings for his crew had been slim. "I don't think we've worked too much together, have we? Whaddya go by again?"

"First name's Jules, but Laramie's just fine. That's my surname."

To Paul, the man looked like he might fall over on the spot. "Well, Laramie, there isn't a tree I can't bring down, and I intend to take 'em all by springtime. For now, just keep working on this space and the bunkhouse. We'll worry about the rest later." Paul turned to the other men in the clearing, who were starting to erect the border of the rectangular bunkhouse. "I'll be headin' back early tomorrow mornin' to get things finalized and bring the foreman and the rest of the crew up. By early next week, we should be in full swing with a camp cook and all. It's a good time to be chopping trees and tossing logs, boys. Let's hustle up and finish before dark."

A chorus of hollers rose in approval. Paul got caught up in the moment, which seemed like a celebration. His arms swelled, and his chest grew like a rolling thundercloud. *It's good to be out here.*

———

The sky was still dark when Paul woke. He slipped on his boots and walked silently through the woods, watching the sky slowly brighten and the final morning star disappear into daylight. He was moving south quickly, twice as fast as most men could on horseback. He was fueled by the upcoming season of logging and felt no hunger for food nor thirst for drink. All Paul needed to sustain himself was Amelia and the adrenaline-filled weight of his ax.

By late morning, he still had a long way to go. The sun was high, and the morning chill was long gone. He knew it took two days of travel for most men, but figured that without being held up by the others, he could get back by nightfall, hoping to see Amelia and ease the tension that he had left between them.

Paul came across many creatures during his trip back, much more than usual. Chipmunks and squirrels skittered past his feet, led by black-capped chickadees and woodpeckers. Nearly all of them seemed to be heading in the opposite direction.

Even for Paul, who was by no means an expert about the animals of the woods, it was a little odd to see so many critters out and about. The first and only animal to run with him towards Hinckley was the familiar gray rabbit with the rusty patch of fur behind its neck.

"What are you doin' here, then? Go on, get outta here." Paul whipped a pine cone at its tail, but it dodged the projectile easily. It sped up faster than lightning and darted in and out of the piles of slash and shrubbery in front of him. About every five minutes or so, Paul caught a glimpse of the rabbit sitting with a patient expression, waiting for him to catch up. Each time, the animal immediately turned and ran ahead of him, just out of sight.

As the sun began descending from its summit, Paul started to notice more and more birds flying and beasts running in the opposite direction: herons, eagles, grouse, chipmunks, squirrels, pine marten, and an innumerable number of songbirds. It was a strange scene that only became odder the closer he got to Hinckley. It was no longer just birds and rodents scurrying past. Paul nearly ran into a pack of six or seven wolves and a herd of caribou who didn't stop to glance at the tall man jumping out of their way.

The surreal parade of animals made him anxious. When the wind picked up and blew the first hot, dry scent of sweet, smoky pine, Paul's eyes widened. He stopped dead in his tracks and watched as a single, dirty snowflake swirled like the first sign of a winter flurry onto his shirt. He reached to his chest and gently picked up the piece of ash, then watched it turn to powder as he rubbed it between his thumb and forefinger.

Paul's heart began pumping like the piston of a steam engine, and his stomach felt tight and sick as he raced along the uneven road that led south next to the logging railway. He figured he was still about eight or ten miles out of Hinckley, but he needed to be there now. He no longer saw the piles of slash and animals flying past him. All Paul saw were the images from his strange dream: the rabbit, the man, and Amelia cloaked in flames.

———

That summer, the tall, blond-haired American Swede known to pretty much everyone in town as Ola had come up from St. Paul to spend the warm months working the lumber mills in Hinckley. Unfortunately, instead of making a name for himself as a successful lumberjack as he had hoped, he became known as the town drunk and the punchline of many jokes. Ola spent more time in the saloons spinning yarns than he did working toward a paycheck, but he was generally kind and rarely showed a temper unless he was nearing his limit of whiskey.

On the morning of the first of September, he was working off a particularly severe headache from the previous night's escapades. Ola's temples pounded with each heartbeat, and his right eye was nearly swollen shut and, he presumed, turning a deep shade of violet. He was preparing himself for a miserable day when he found an unused cigarette stuck between the floorboards outside the saloon where he had spent the night. Using a small stick, he lifted the papery smoke from its grave. By the uniform, tight roll of the tobacco, Ola figured it must have fallen from the carrying case of a well-to-do somebody.

"Probably that good-for-nothing Brennen. Bet he smokes something like this," he mumbled as he turned the cigarette over in his hands. He held it with the same care one would have if they were holding a precious jewel. Ola passed the slender, paper-wrapped stick under his nose. "Oh my. My day might just be looking up." He slid the cigarette behind his ear and walked down the street to stroll along the train tracks.

As Ola stepped alongside the iron rails, he took out a small box of matches and went through a few broken sticks before he finally got one to light. He held the flame to the tip of the cigarette and took a long, slow drag. Holding his breath, he thought to himself, *I was right. This is a good smoke.*

Ola walked by the tracks, savoring the sweet tobacco. He admired the velvety clusters on the sumac shrubs and the bulging pods of the milkweed lining the ditch. He was thinking about leaving Hinckley. The summer hadn't been as productive as he had hoped. It had been sweltering hot and very dry, so dry, in fact, that fires had been sparking up here and there outside of town. But when it came down to it, he was just plain bored of the country and longed for the lively action of the city. St. Paul had kept his distracted mind in check. Here, Ola was left to wander, and most often, he found that his feet led him to the closest saloon and its friendliest smooth-skinned host. It wasn't necessarily a bad thing, but he had already more than exhausted the options available to him so that even the evening company was becoming mundane.

Ola continued strolling along until he came to the decision that it was indeed time to leave this town. And if he was going to leave, why wait any longer? He knew a train would be heading through in the early afternoon. Ready to get back to pack and settle any outstanding debts, he struck one more match to finish off the butt of the cigarette and flicked the matchstick over the tracks. Ola took one final puff. "Might even have time for a quick drink before I go," he said to himself.

Whistling an upbeat melody, Ola closed his eyes and enjoyed the warm breeze from the southwest, not noticing the small wisp of smoke just visible from the resting place of the match used to finish off his lucky cigarette.

————

The sky was ablaze. A sunset well before nightfall was on the horizon, and Paul was running into a wall of heat. Ashes floated past him like cottonwood seeds. As he got closer to town, the ashes turned to embers and his clothes began to feel hot and dry against his skin despite the sweat he'd been swimming in.

When Paul finally pushed over the hill looking toward town, he came to a halt. The flames were climbing trees and leaping a hundred feet in the air. The heat hit his face like a bag of heavy sand, and his eyes flooded with water in response. He followed the railroad tracks into town but had to veer off as he approached Brennen's mill. As he came closer, the dancing fire lunged viciously, looking to swallow anything in its vicinity with a supernatural fury.

Paul weaved through remnants of smoldering homes composed of piles of charcoal and collapsed chimneys and found himself by the lake. People were clinging to each other in the water, some choking on smoke, some floating facedown. The roar of the fire around him drowned out the sounds of screaming and crying. The pale bellies of fish bobbed at the surface as the water began to steam. Paul scanned the water but couldn't hear or see Amelia Brennen.

His hair was singed as he ran back to the train depot, where he found Otto helping close the doors on the last car as the train huffed and puffed, ready to flee.

"Otto! Where's Amelia!?" Paul grabbed him hard, spinning the large man around like a top.

Relief spread across Otto's face at the sight of Paul. "Paul! I thought you were up north! You have to get out of here, my friend. Come with us. The train is leaving." Otto had blisters on his hands and soot smudged across his face, and his shirt sleeves were singed at the edges from combing the fire for survivors. The wheels of the train started spinning, and it creaked forward.

"I need to find Amelia! The mill is gone, and I didn't see her in the lake. Have ya seen her, Otto?" he frantically pleaded.

"Paul, we have to go now. I'm sure she got out."

"Is she on this train? Did she get on the train?!" Paul shouted.

"I didn't see her, but you need to get out, my friend. We will all die if we stay much longer!"

The flames were licking the clouds and roaring like the steam engine at their side. Paul and Otto could barely hear each other. It was as if the gate to hell had opened up and its contents had erupted on Hinckley. The fire was inhaling all of the air around them.

"I'm going back to find her!" Paul yelled as he turned away from Otto.

Otto reached for Paul's arm, but Paul pulled away, barely noticing the attempt to restrain him, and ran. The heat was unbearable. He could smell his hair burning and feel his skin searing, and he didn't need to look at his arms to know that blisters were beginning to bubble up.

"AMELIA!!!" Paul shouted over and over. He couldn't recognize the buildings or roads any longer. He was surrounded by flames.

"AMELIA!!!" Paul's throat was burning from the screaming and the heat. He began to cough. He didn't hear or feel Otto yelling at him and pulling him back. He kept trying to move forward into the jaws of the flames that were coming to meet him. Otto was pulling and shouting with all his might, but his massive friend was too strong for him.

Was he always this big?! Otto thought.

In a moment of final desperation, Otto saw a shovel lying nearby on the ground, picked it up, and swung it as hard as he could, coming down on the crown of his friend's head. Paul toppled over into the dirt like the countless trees that had fallen by his hands. The flames were gaining speed, ready to engulf them both. Otto used every ounce of strength to lift the dead weight of the giant over his shoulder and ran to catch the last train car pulling out of the town that once was Hinckley, Minnesota.

———

It took seven hours for Paul to wake up. The firestorm had lasted only four, but it had burned nearly 400 square miles, leaving Hinckley and five other towns in piles of charcoal and ash. The smell of death and destruction hung in the smoky air.

Paul's brain buzzed with a high-pitched vibration. It took him several minutes to realize that it wasn't coming from between his ears, but from the world around him. The evening's choir of crickets was singing loudly for anyone who would listen.

He opened his eyes into the darkness. He felt the hard wooden floor under him. An empty doorframe near his feet was lit by the moonlight, and the sounds of hurried footsteps and anxious voices surrounded him.

As Paul's eyes began to adjust to the light, he sat up. He let out a moan as each of the hundreds of cuts and blisters covering his body screamed with every movement.

"Where am I?" he groaned. Looking around, Paul made out the empty train car. Even in the darkness, he could see his burned shirt. His skin was taut and red as a ripe tomato. Taking a deep breath and stopping sharply due to the discomfort, he inhaled the strong smell of smoke.

When the scent registered in his mind, it was as if he had fallen through the ice of a frozen lake. In an instant, the day's events raced back to him, spinning in a dizzy whirlwind of flames and pain.

"Amelia!" he shouted. Paul jumped up, hitting his head on the roof of the train car, and let out a growl. He ducked through the door and stepped out into the night, looking around to get his bearings. Paul grabbed the nearest person he could find and spun them around to face him. His eyes met the familiar foolish face of Ola Värmlänning. "Where are we?!" he asked.

Ola looked at Paul quizzically. "Skunk Lake, Paul. Didn't you ride the train with the rest of us?"

"Amelia Brennen. Ola, have ya seen Amelia Brennen?" Paul was still as a statue and fixed on Ola's face. The Swede swayed back and forth, blinking slowly. Paul could see him searching his memory, looking for the name "Brennen" in his mental attic.

Ola's face turned to a scowl. "You mean Patrick Brennen? That son of a gun who kicked me out of his mill? Don't know who he thinks he is telling me I'm..."

"No! Amelia. Amelia Brennen. His daughter. Have you seen her?" Paul spoke each of the last words slowly and clearly to try and break through the rambling man's trance. Every muscle in his body was flexed and tense like a bowstring as he waited for the answer.

"Oh! Amelia Brennen." The Swede's face brightened. "Oh, she's a pretty one, Paul, she is, for sure....No, I don't think I've seen her. Most of the folks are camping somewhere near the front of the train, though. You could check up there, I suppose."

Ola continued speaking as Paul turned and jogged up the train, scanning the small groups of people sitting, huddled up, some crying, others sleeping alongside the tracks. He searched and searched, stopping to ask familiar faces if they had seen any of the Brennens. Paul's panic was snowballing. His pace picked up.

Whenever Paul looked back on that night in the years to come, he remembered it only as a flurry of soot-filled faces sharing the same blank expression of shock and tragedy with no sign of the one face he needed to see most. The face of a beautiful girl with dark eyes, chestnut hair, and a soft smile that could bring the tallest tree to its knees.

———

Paul found Otto helping distribute food and water to folks near the back side of the train depot. The two caught sight of each other, and Paul looked to Otto's face for any sign of good news. His friend shook his head.

"Paul, I haven't seen her. I've looked all over. No one has," Otto said.

The fire was still raging, this time in Paul's veins. His stomach felt as if someone was clenching his innards with their fist.

"Otto, you're sure?" Paul finally asked.

Otto nodded, but said nothing.

Paul turned and ran as he had never run before. The doors of the train cars rattled as he sped past, and each footfall left a small crater behind him. He leapt over a small group of people sitting on the ground, feeling his muscles swell with sickening rage and fear of what he might find when he got to whatever remained of Hinckley. The five miles were smoky, hot, and dark, and Paul flew through the land at a blistering pace. Though he probably covered the distance in twenty to thirty minutes, it felt like an eternity.

He came to a massive swath of embers, the remnants of smoldering houses and buildings, which gave the night an eerie glow. Heat radiated from the ground. All around him, Paul could hear soft cracking, hissing, and popping sounds. He coughed as he raced through the town. It felt like he was walking through water as he trudged through the unrecognizable world.

When Paul came upon a large pile of burning wood and melted metal, he recognized the warped saw blades from Brennen's mill. He looked around pleadingly for any sign of life. "Amelia!" he shouted. He called out her name again and again.

A soft shuffle from behind him made him spin around. For a moment, he truly thought he might see his lover, but there, next to a small tarnished piece of metal half-buried in the ash-covered ground, was the rabbit who ran ahead of him earlier in the day.

Paul didn't know how or why, but he felt like this animal was to blame for all of the carnage. Rage welled up from somewhere deep within him. He hated this small beast that taunted him in this smoldering wasteland.

"You! What do you want from me!? Get out of here!" Paul screamed. He searched for anything he could throw at the rabbit. An iron rod sat near his feet, twisted by the fire. It seared his palm as he grabbed it and heaved it at the animal. The rabbit darted out of the way and sped off as the projectile hit the ground, kicking up a cloud of debris. In the settling dust where the rabbit once sat, a glint of gold caught Paul's eye. He walked over to the tiny metal object.

As Paul reached to pick it up, the blood emptied from his heart. His body went numb as he closed his fingers on the blackened, deformed locket, misshapen from the heat. In spite of the appearance, Paul knew it was the same locket that used to rest in the hollow of Amelia's neck. It was still closed, the clasp intact. He didn't want to see what he already knew was inside, but he couldn't stop himself from opening it. Gently lifting the clasp, Paul's gaze rested on a small photograph. The edges were singed and flaking away, but the image was mostly preserved. Paul looked at the face of a young, dark-haired boy. A boy who was innocent to the loss of his parents. A boy who could barely contain his excitement. A boy who was naive to romantic love. A boy who knew nothing of pain. But now, the anguish was falling as hard and heavy as all the trees Paul had ever logged. He collapsed to his knees. Holding the locket to his chest, he wept uncontrollably.

Years later, children would speak of Paul Bunyan and his many feats of strength. They would talk of how the lakes of Minnesota were made from his giant footsteps. But to Paul, those lakes were made from the tears he shed for Amelia Brennen on the night of September 1, 1894.

The great Lake Superior is said to wear many emotions. On warm summer days, her glassy waters invite children to bathe in her pools as she rests like a newborn lamb. Under the pressure of a winter storm, she swells with rage and hammers the shores in anger, challenging anyone to sail her waters. And when she wears a cloak of fog like a cold, deep depression, it's because Paul's tears of sadness have found their way back to the water's surface.

Gathering Ashes, 1894

Every ash
Falling on me
Will
Eventually
Become a falling leaf.

Four hundred and eighteen. That was the estimated number of lives lost in the Hinckley fire. Family members and lovers. Friends and strangers. Criminals and saints. All of them worth saving. Each a senseless loss. For many survivors, a mixture of guilt and gratitude kept them afloat as they rebuilt their lives.

For Paul, sour hatred filled him to the point that it began seeping out of his pores. He spent the first few days after the disaster camping at the boundary of the fire, watching the remaining embers late into the night. It took days for the coals to extinguish. He fought sleep as much as possible since every moment of it was spent reliving his last sight of Amelia and her unending cries for help.

On the fourth night, he followed the same routine, fighting sleep with every ounce of strength he could muster. His body gave out in the hours just past midnight and slipped into the same painful dream. Amelia stood in front of Paul, looking right at him, seeing more of him than he was willing to share. Even in the dream, her presence made him feel childish and exposed with her omniscient glances. And once again, flames eventually engulfed her and cries spun around his head, but her smile never left her face.

Something was different about the crying this time. Buried deep in the dream, Paul hung onto a small thread of consciousness still aware enough to acknowledge the difference in the wailing. He knew the cry was real. It was coming from outside his mind and body. He clung to the sound like a long rope as it lifted him from the deep water of his dream. Then he opened his eyes to the dark morning and a bleating call coming from somewhere nearby.

Paul staggered to his feet and began to follow the sound. About a hundred yards off, he found the source. A thin-legged caribou calf was caught in a length of wire fencing. The animal was struggling to stand, let alone get free. Its call was one of despair and fright.

When it saw Paul coming closer, it began to kick and thrash, attempting to escape, but the weak beanstalk legs battled the wire fruitlessly and buckled under the animal's weight.

"Easy there, now. I ain't gonna hurt ya." Paul edged closer, hands low but outstretched. Slowly, he ran his fingers down the calf's hind leg and loosened the wire. The animal stumbled free and fell to the ground. "There ya go," he said, backing away. The caribou tried to stand a few times, but finally gave up. It looked up to Paul with sagging eyelids. Blinking one last, slow blink, it closed its golden eyes and curled into an exhausted heap of bones and fur.

Paul stood motionless, debating what to do. Finally, he stepped forward and bent down to lift the bony animal into his arms. He cradled it gently and walked it back to his camp, where he spent the next few days trying to get the animal to drink water and, eventually, eat.

That was how Otto found Paul, sitting next to a pile of debris cleared from the nearby road, feeding clover flowers to a young animal.

"Where'd you get him?" Otto asked, gesturing to the small, sickly creature. "He doesn't look too good."

"Found him over in the woods trapped in some fencing. Didn't think he would've made it if I'da left him," Paul said. He didn't look at his friend, who was staring intensely at him. Otto was afraid of what would happen to Paul if he left him there much longer.

"Paul, some of us are heading north where they're hiring. Now that Mr. Brennen's…" Otto paused briefly at the mention of Brennen's name, but recovered quickly and continued, "Now that the mill is gone, there's more timber to collect for the other companies. You…you want to join?"

Paul sat, stroking the rough, gray hairs on the animal's back, his fingertips rolling up and down over the protruding vertebrae. "I think I'm gonna keep him," he said.

Otto was caught off guard. "The caribou? Why?"

"I think he'll be a good worker. We used to have an ox. My parents, I mean. A strong one too. Hauled our wagon nearly halfway across the country. We named her Mama because she always took care of us." Paul chuckled. "Made for some confusing times when I was talking with Pa. 'Hey Pa! Mama's loose again!' He'd look at me all confused, half expecting to see his wife running out of the house in nothing but her nightgown." He began laughing so hard that tears streamed down his face.

After a few moments, Paul sighed, wiping the tears away and catching his breath. "If that ox was Mama, I'm gonna call you Babe… what do ya think, Otto?"

"You're naming the caribou?" Otto knew people did strange things when they had been through stressful experiences, but this seemed a little odder than usual. "I think you need to come up north with me, Paul. Get back to work, you know? Get back to doing what you love." He hesitated. "I know it must be hard, losing Amelia."

"Don't say her name!" Paul shouted. His smile gone, he closed his eyes as if he knew there would only be a few more chances to hear her name and see her face. Paul didn't want to waste one on this moment.

The massive lumberjack sat, eyes closed, his hand resting on the animal's neck, who was now munching some grass. Babe was about as weak as a bundle of wet clothes, but at least he was eating.

The skin on Paul's hands was peeling from the burns. His physical aches and pains were all but gone, but the internal anguish was still present in full force. Paul sighed, opened his eyes, and said, "I'll come."

"Alright then. We're leaving tomorrow around mid-morning if you want to join us for the journey. And Paul..." Otto had started to walk away but stopped with a concerned look at the bony mass of fur at Paul's side. The pathetic animal did not look long for this world. "Consider leaving the caribou, er, a, Babe. I mean, I don't think he'll make it much longer by the looks of him."

Paul gave a soft noise in response, which didn't reveal any agreement on the matter. He kept his eyes on the calf. It was comforting to feel the touch of another living thing. Paul never thought of himself as an emotional or physical person, but rather that he was following in the footsteps of his father. His mother had a way of breaking through his walls, but it wasn't until he met Amelia that his guard started breaking down completely. She could move into his space with ease, like the way spring quietly puts winter to sleep. He'd felt a completeness and satisfaction he'd never known until he met her. It was as if Paul had been walking around his entire life missing a piece of his body, and he'd finally found it only to have it ripped away from him in a shower of flames and anguish. The calf didn't replace that, but Paul felt comforted by the beast all the same. The two were just fragile enough to need each other in spite of their mutual independence and wildness. The decision was made. Babe would be making the journey.

Otto left the pair sitting by the road. Paul laid his head down on his rucksack and closed his eyes. Babe finished the pile of greens and shifted his position to rest his chin on the belly of the tall man who, in turn, absentmindedly rested his hand behind the fuzzy ears. To their left was the fire line and beyond that a blackened space filled with death. To the right was a world untouched by the firestorm. The small pines and scattered maples and aspens were starting to consider the colors of autumn. On the border of the two worlds, Paul and Babe fell into a deep sleep and rested well for the first time in days.

———

The troop of men made their way up north, slowly dispersing as work was found here and there. Soon enough, it was just Otto, Paul, and Babe moving on to the most isolated logging camps.

It had only been a couple weeks since the fire, but the weather was changing quickly. Late September was a friend to the aspen leaves. The mixture of brilliant yellows, greens, and oranges sprinkled the hillsides and were a stark contrast to the dark, feathery green pines and gray granite rocks frosted with colorful lichens. The ground was coated in the sweet smell of wet, rotting leaves, and most mornings, a diamond blanket of frost covered their world.

"Over here now, Babe. Gotta fix that pack before it slides off ya." The animal happily trotted up to Paul, who adjusted the rucksacks and Otto's long saw on the creature's back.

Babe had grown substantially in the last three weeks. It was shocking, really. "Look at him. His back is up to your waist, Paul." Otto had given up being surprised by the waxing and waning of his friend's height, which, after shrinking throughout the summer, seemed to be on the upswing, but the caribou was different. It was alarming how large he'd grown in such a short amount of time. He wondered if there was a deeper connection between Paul and the animal than he had initially thought.

"Not sure what to tell you, Otto. Takes after me I guess, don't ya, Babe?" Babe gave a snort and a headshake in reply, and Paul laughed.

Otto wasn't sure how Babe would do in the logging camps, but whatever healing Paul needed from Amelia's death, it was clear that Babe was going to be a big piece of it. Otto watched his friend brush some debris off Babe's coarse, gray coat of fur.

The trees around them began to whisper in the breeze. Paul's hair was getting longer, and it came awake in the wind. The crisp autumn air was refreshing. It didn't yet carry the sharp smell of winter, but instead held the last scraps of summer, hoping for one more dance. The air washed clean the frequent nightmares filled with flames and pain plaguing Paul's sleep. Otto didn't ask Paul about the dreams, but twice now he had to shake Paul awake from his nightmarish thrashing, swinging, and screaming about fire, Amelia, and a rabbit.

Their pace was casual. Slow. They lingered near the small lakes and streams that dotted the landscape. The nights were a spectacle of stars and flowing colors. Three nights straight, they were treated to a show of emerald and rose-colored wisps undulating through the sky like a curtain hanging over an open kitchen window.

"Whaddya think those lights are?" Paul lay on his back on a large piece of granite at the lakeshore, Babe resting behind him.

Otto didn't respond immediately. This was the first time in a while that Paul had talked to him about a topic other than their day-to-day travel. Otto sat, filing the teeth of his saw. Usually, he had it strapped across his back while traveling, but their animal friend had been carrying it, giving him a nice reprieve.

"Well...not quite sure exactly. I've heard that the Ojibwe think they're dancing spirits. Their ancestors moving on to the next life." Paul didn't respond. "But I don't know...maybe they don't mean anything. Maybe they're just pretty to look at the same way a sunset is or these lakes are in the morning."

Paul shifted on the ground and cleared his throat. For a moment, the only sound was Babe's slow, heavy breathing. Finally, he spoke.

"Yeah. Who knows what they are? Sometimes they look like fire, and sometimes they look like the water that puts the fire out." Paul made a noise as if he were going to continue along this train of thought, but he stopped abruptly. Otto had an idea where Paul was heading but decided to sit quietly, waiting for Paul to go on.

"Do ya think people ever get over loss and the pain that comes with it?" Paul asked.

Babe's rhythmic breathing seemed to be conducting the dancing lights. Otto took a deep breath before responding. "No. I do not. Not completely, anyway. I've got scars on my arms that don't hurt like the cuts that caused them, but the memory is still there. Like these lights. They'll burn out tonight, but we'll still see them when we close our eyes."

"Mm-hmm." Paul's reply was soft and weak, the sound of a broken man unsure of what to do next.

They sat for close to an hour watching the lights. Otto knew Paul was still awake. He feared that if he didn't get him moving soon, the man would sink away into a place too far gone. It was time to get him logging again. "I think we should try to get to a camp and start working, Paul. We need food and a roof over our heads, and I'm ready to get cutting again. How about you?"

Paul didn't make a sound. His breathing seemed to have stopped.

Babe, too, was no longer sleeping and had raised his head to check on his companion. Paul sat up for a moment, then got to his feet. He inhaled deeply. As he fully expanded his chest, he seemed to stretch a few inches taller, bones groaning like a knotty oak swaying in the wind.

"Okay," he said. He turned and walked back to the softer ground covered by leaves, pine straw, and moss to get some sleep beneath the trees. Babe followed, leaving Otto alone at the rocky lakeshore.

It was a relief to hear Paul comply. He rarely followed the instructions of others so willingly. In the time Otto had known Paul, he had been a man who preferred to work alone, as if the feeling of completing a task without help fueled him and made him stronger. The fact that he was willing to go without any protest or input said a lot about the despair he must have felt. Otto knew his friend was struggling immensely. Paul had found a companion in Babe, but now he needed to get back to work. He needed to swing his ax.

———

After a short night's sleep, they broke camp and set off early the next morning. By midday, they had found their way into a small logging town filled with the busy comings and goings of people getting ready for winter. Heads turned and eyes lingered on the strange visitors. It was, after all, quite a sight: two large men, one towering over the other, and a caribou alongside to boot. Rumors spread like wildfire, so it wasn't long before the entire town knew that Big Paul Bunyan was in their midst. This turned out to be rather helpful. Paul and Otto didn't need to look for work. The work found them.

After some lengthy discussions and a few ultimatums, they found a logging company that would not only get them straight to work but also tolerated Babe tagging along. Paul knew the animal would be a phenomenal force in the woods and made sure to sell him that way.

"I know his legs look skinny, but trust me," Paul told the man in charge of recruiting loggers, who was looking skeptically at the gangly creature. "He'll pull twice as much as any team of oxen you've got and eat half. If he doesn't, you can cut my wages." Paul grinned at Babe and tousled the animal's fur, feeling the two stubby antlers sprouting next to his ears.

Otto struggled to hide his pleasure in seeing his friend show a spark of giddy excitement. Even Babe seemed to be a bit more playful as they made their way farther north to camp. The caribou would launch up the trail, kicking off tree stumps and spinning in circles like a carefree puppy as Otto and Paul laughed.

By the time they walked into camp, Paul felt a small spark of hope that brighter days may be burning deep inside him. The ember was still surrounded by the dark emptiness of loss and pain, but if he pushed those feelings aside and built a wall tall enough to keep them at bay, he could focus on the forest and the smells and sounds of the logging camp. He just might start to feel whole again after all.

"This is gonna be good, Otto," he said to himself as much as his friend as they made their way to the shanty where the men were gathering before dinner. Word that they'd be joining had come ahead of them, but no advance notice could have prepared the loggers for the sight of the two towering lumberjacks walking into camp trailed by a harnessed caribou. They stared wide-eyed at the trio, whispers of recognition spreading among them.

After a short discussion with the foreman, the newcomers had their provisions negotiated and sleeping quarters arranged. That night, they feasted on pine beef and cakes, then made their way to the corner of the bunkhouse where the largest bunks were.

"Tomorrow, Otto, the work starts. You ready?" Paul asked. He was lying down with his hands behind his head and his eyes closed, imagining the tall trees that awaited their sentence. His bones ached for the chance to bring them down. Trees six feet across filled with sticky sap waited to be tapped.

"I can feel the acres of old pines just outside that door," Otto said. "I'm as ready as you are. But first, I want to sleep. It's been too long since we've been in a bed. Don't you agree? Paul? Where are you going?"

Paul had stood up and was tightening his shoelaces. "On second thought," he said, "I'm not quite ready to lie down. Gonna sharpen my ax a bit by the fire. Rest up, Otto." Paul threw on an ashen wool cap and grabbed his ax. He weaved through the crowded bunkhouse and ducked out the doorway.

"Suit yourself," Otto called as he rolled over and quickly drifted off to sleep while the rest of the lumberjacks in the bunkhouse joked and sang songs and told tales of paddling down rivers on the backs of large bull moose.

Outside at the fire, Paul sat sharpening his ax, watching the flames waltz back and forth. Inside the blue, white, and orange tongues leaping up to the moonlight, he couldn't ignore the faces of his mother, father, and Amelia. The cold sharpening stone made a rhythmic swipe as it slid across the blade, occasionally shooting off sparks into the darkness.

Nearby, just beyond the reach of the firelight, a small rabbit watched the tall man hunched over the fire. The rabbit's nose twitched. It watched the big shoulders slowly rise and fall as the man breathed in and out. The weight of loss was piling up on the man's shoulders like large slabs of granite, but also growing was the determination to close himself off to pain and claim a forest as his own. This man was set on one goal: to swing and haul as no man had done before. The rabbit smelled a fermenting, sour mix of anger and sadness welling deep in the man's heart, and with each contraction of the big, empty muscle, grief and rage mixed into a volatile cocktail, filling his body. The only way for him to keep it at bay was to swing that silver ax and swing it hard. And swing it he would. The rabbit knew these lands would continue to change, but it hoped that someday the pines would grow old again and its people would return. And with the images of clear-cut forests flashing in its mind, the rabbit turned and hopped away into the night.

Anniversary: 1895

Into the forest, I will go
Where the leaves and the needles cover the stones
Little creatures call the ground their home
Lay me down until the lichen grows
Into the forest, I will go
I will not be alone

If ever there was truth behind the legendary tales of Paul Cunningham, or "Bunyan" as you may know him, the stories likely came from this period of Paul's life. Never before had a man swung an ax as hard or true as Paul in those days. To Paul, the trees were made to fall, and he had been delivered by a storm to bring them down.

With Babe at his side, Paul became a logging force the likes of which had never been seen. He fashioned a harness of old leather straps to slide over Babe's nose and ears, and Babe, who had grown to nearly twice the size of a typical caribou, hauled loads in his single oxen harness down to the railway while Paul directed him with a long set of reins. When he didn't need the reins, Paul wrapped them tightly around Babe's antlers, and once Babe got the hang of finding the railway, Paul let him haul on his own so he could return to swinging his ax deep into the torsos of the tall trees. It was as if each day spent swinging his ax made Paul's muscles swell and his bones grow. He must have been seven or eight feet tall by then, and his baritone voice was like a booming locomotive.

Babe had made a name for himself as well, not only due to his size but also in color. His coat held hints of cream, silver, and walnut. In the darkness, his chocolate-colored eyes reflected golden light except when the long nights of winter arrived. When the sun began to stay down more than up, the shine in his eyes turned to a deep, shimmering blue, and thus it was that the shanty men started calling him "Babe the Blue" because of the cool sapphire eyes shining from the edges of camp on long winter evenings.

In spite of, or possibly because of, the unbelievable feats of strength Paul and Babe performed almost weekly, there was an edge of apprehension among the men when working around Paul. His ax swung with an undertone of madness, and his temper was quick to wake. His near ferocity began to crescendo as summer ended and September approached.

As the anniversary of the Hinckley fire approached, Paul was seen less and less. He and Babe would chop and haul timber until sunrise, resting a few hours in the morning far from camp only to wake and begin working again. Maybe it was the proximity of the two, but Babe seemed to take on the personality of his friend, snorting and shaking his antlers at anyone who might get in the way of their day's work. A few of the men even swore that Babe snarled at them when they got too close, but they, of course, didn't dare raise a complaint.

No one spoke of them, and when the first day of September finally came, the two were nowhere to be found. Even Otto, who now spent most of his time with the other loggers and little time with Paul, didn't know and dared not ask where his friend had gone.

Somewhere deep in the woods, Paul and Babe spent the day walking up a small stone creek bed. The water was the color of dark tea, stained from the seeping tannins of the forest floor. They walked past brambles of cut tree limbs and new undergrowth, aspens and even a few maples, and startled a small group of white-tailed deer munching on young pine saplings. Paul didn't remember seeing deer this far north, but it seemed more and more common lately. Babe eyed them cautiously as they leapt away, tails high in the air like flagpoles calling the alarm on the intruders.

The two hiked further and further until they reached a massive crisscross of logs damming the stream. Spurts of water trickled down to form the small creek they had been following. A still, glassy pond rested at eye level in front of them, only disrupted by a tiny, furry head silently swimming in the distance. The beaver spotted them, slapped its tail, and dove under the water.

Paul looked at the piled-up logs. They made a home for this animal and its family. They provided a haven for its loved ones and a place to store food all winter. Even on the most frigid nights when temperatures could cause a tree to explode from the freezing sap, the family of beavers would be warm and cozy inside, munching on their cache of sticks and twigs.

A small trout rose to the surface in the middle of the pond, sending a succession of small rings rippling through the water. The beavers had created a refuge here. Neither wolf nor mountain lion would be able to threaten them. They had the perfect little home, and Paul hated them for it.

He hated that these animals could live in their peace and happiness while he was sentenced to isolation and anguish all because of some freakish accident. His temples began to pound, and his blood was coming to a boil. His fist clenched the handle of his large ax. His vision clouded as the hate for the dam, the beavers, the pines, the deer, all of it grew. The last straw was the sight of the rabbit hopping along the far edge of the pond, stopping to stare directly at Paul.

"YOU! What are you?!" Paul shouted. He grabbed his ax with both hands and swung it upwards through the center of the dam. Babe made a bleating grunt and jumped back. The dam burst open, and half-chewed sticks and mud flew through the air.

Water rushed across Paul's body, slamming him against the rocks of the streambed where he managed to roll onto his stomach and cover his head. His ears filled with the harsh thrill of rushing water moving all around him. When he felt the pressure of the water give, he forced himself to his feet and stared down the stream that was now restored to its original size. Water dripped down his face. Paul breathed heavily as he walked out of the stream.

"C'mon, Babe," he said without looking at his friend. He walked along the bank of the stream, heading back the way they came, pushing from his mind the squeaks of the beaver's pups that had just lost their home. Babe glanced at the emptying pond, then reluctantly turned to follow. Paul didn't look back to see if the rabbit was still there. He didn't want to know.

That day, as the water returned to the creek and flowed past the camp with Paul and Babe walking alongside, stories spread of how Paul dug the entire river with his ax. In neighboring towns, the rivers turned into lakes. Out East and out West, those lakes became canyons and mountains. Paul Bunyan could do anything.

Friends, After 1895

When the night is at its darkest
And the moon is far from home,
Will you sit with me in silence
So I will not be alone?
I know this will not last forever
And your company will fade,
But while you're by my side
I am thankful for this place.

Otto was sitting in camp near a couple of the German sawmen, enjoying his nightly ritual of sharpening his saw in preparation for another day of work. Even though his hands were quick, it still took a good half hour to file every tooth of the blade. While he sharpened his saw, he liked to imagine that he was filing the treacherous jaws of an enormous timber wolf. Otto looked up to see Paul walking his way and slid to the side to give his friend room to sit down beside him.

The wooden bench bent and creaked under the weight of the two friends. Paul looked across the fire to the Germans, who finished their conversation and left for the bunkhouse, then sat quietly watching the fire, listening to the metal-on-metal scraping of Otto's file and saw. This year of logging hadn't been the return to glory either of the men had hoped they would find. It had been bitter and lonely.

Paul sighed and looked up to the dark sky. "Otto, I'm thinking of moving on a bit. With winter on its way, I'd like to get on to a new camp with some fresh trees. Interested in joining me?" It had been a week since he had walked back down the streambed, and it was the first time he had spoken to Otto in nearly a month.

Otto nodded. "I could do that. Is it just new trees you're looking for?" He always found it easy to slip into casual conversation with Paul, no matter the tall man's mood.

"Well, ya know, Babe could use a change of scenery, and these men are starting to get on my nerves with all their stories and such. And I just don't know if I can stand another winter here in the shanty with them and all their lice. Some of these boys are practically family with the critters." This was the closest thing to a joke that Otto had heard from his friend in nearly a year. The playful banter was fragile but a good sign.

"Well, you know me," Otto said. "I'm always up for an adventure, my friend."

"So that's a yes?" There was a hopeful hesitation in Paul's tone.

"Sure," Otto replied. "Why not? It's been feeling a little slow here lately. I mean, I hate to say it, but I believe you've been losing your touch. I've been out-sawing you for months now."

"Oh-ho! Is that so, then?" Paul came to life at the slight. "Well, looks like we'll just have to make a few wagers along the way to the next camp and see who really is the best up here in these woods." The two laughed and spent the rest of the evening chuckling about the new recruits in camp and the pranks that were played on them. They'd seen enough men get laxatives slipped into their drinks to scare the devil himself out of sipping tea. They didn't need to stick around to see a few more men rushing out of the bunkhouse in frigid temperatures holding their heinies.

By the end of the week, Otto and Paul had squared up with the camp boss. The man in charge made it more than clear how unhappy he was that they were leaving, but he didn't go so far as to say they couldn't come back.

"When you two get back from your fool's errand, I just might be able to find a spot for you again, if you're lucky. But don't take too long. Winter'll be here soon enough," said the foreman.

Otto and Paul nodded in thanks and turned to walk out of camp, following the road north. Babe had their packs balanced on each side of his body and trotted behind the two men. Otto's saw lay across Babe's back, reaching out like the wings of a heron, but Paul carried his ax, resting it over his shoulder. The season's first frost crunched beneath their feet, filling the conversationless void in the early hours of the morning before the layer of crystals melted away.

Trudging through the uncut forest gave the two opportunities to enjoy a few friendly logging challenges.

"On the count of three," Paul called to Otto as they stood by their chosen trees, ready to see who could bring theirs down the fastest. "One. Two. Three!"

Wood chips and sawdust flew through the air mixed with rhythmic chopping and sawing. This time, Otto's tree hit the ground first.

"Look at that! Your tree was rotten, and you know it!" Paul jeered.

"Your sight seems to be going along with your skill, my friend," Otto fired back. "This tree is as solid as they come."

"I doubt that." Paul laughed and slapped his friend on the back. "Come on. Let's race again." He pointed to another set of trees, and they set off.

Fall called it quits when the first blizzard of the season swung through. Storm or no, the two men kept chopping their way to a lumber company that supposedly was hiring. Not too far from the two lumberjacks, a black-capped chickadee huddled in the branches of a small spruce, trying to disappear into the boughs as the wind raced around it. Its head was tucked down, eyes closed, as it faced the storm. There was no question as to whether the blizzard would end, only if the bird would still be alive by the time the freezing gusts died down. It opened one eye to watch Paul win the latest contest.

"Well, if I don't let you win once in a while, you'll never want to race me again," Otto said. The two were covered in snow from beard to britches.

The competitions and banter were tossed back and forth until they came upon the next company. The foreman of the camp was more than happy to have the extra help. The snow had fallen fast and hard through November and into December, making for slow work.

"Winter is in full swing, boys." The foreman fixed his gaze on Otto and Paul as if hoping to be rescued. "I'll add five dollars to your monthly earnings if you clear our claim by the end of January. We've got nice slick roads for skidding, but this deep snow is keeping us from getting to the trees."

"Heavy snow means a good spring melt, eh?" Paul said, turning to Otto as they walked to claim their place in yet another bunkhouse.

"A heavy melt is useless if there're no logs in the river," said Otto.

"Well, then I guess we better get cutting," Paul replied.

Five dollars a month was more than enough to motivate the two tall loggers. Both men were pushing a hundred trees a day. Paul had Babe to haul his loads, and Otto used a couple teams of horses. The rest of the men in the camp watched in disbelief as the pair of loggers moved through the claim at an astounding rate. They were on track to finish up by mid-January when another big blizzard blew through, dropping over twenty inches of snow and keeping everyone in the bunkhouse for multiple days.

"There's not enough tea and smoke to keep me in here much longer," Paul announced to the group of men, who were all getting cranky and restless after day two indoors. He leaned over and started lacing up his boots.

"You go out there and you'll freeze, Bunyan. We'll find you in a block of ice in a week, and it'll take till spring to thaw you out," the stout camp cook joked as he made his rounds handing out pie to the loggers. "You've got no reason to go out there anyway besides to make your water."

"I hear ya, but I should probably check on Babe soon. He's likely wondering where I am."

"Nah, just stay where you are. I saw him this morning. He's resting in the stables with the other horses. Happy as a pup gnawing on a chicken bone," the cook replied.

Begrudgingly, Paul and Otto stayed put with the other men, who passed the time telling tales of a water lynx living in Lake Superior and a wolf that was split in two then stuck back together again, prowling through northern Wisconsin, and singing songs of women much too good for them. As it always does, the snow finally let up. They woke on the fourth day to blinding sunlight reflecting off every snow-covered surface. After a blizzard like that, it was a struggle to find anything that wasn't covered in snow.

"Keep up, Otto. You're slowing down," Paul called back to the Frenchman. It had taken a couple of days to clear the roads so they could start cutting and hauling again. Babe was made for this type of weather and moved through the snow swiftly. Even Paul, with his big feet that worked almost like snowshoes, managed pretty well. Otto, however, had to take big steps, lifting his knees high in the air to walk through the drifts around each tree, and then took extra time to stomp down a retreat path at its base.

"I'm coming. I'm coming. I do not have those big feet like you. It takes me longer to get where I'm going." Otto's tally had dropped a bit in the days after the snowfall, and Paul had no trouble pointing it out. Despite the snow, they kept cutting and the animals kept hauling, aiming for that January deadline.

"I think we'll be able to finish this tomorrow. That should make the boss happy. Wouldn't ya say?" Paul said to Otto as the two walked back through the woods toward camp in the dimming daylight.

"I would say so. And I will be happy when the days start to grow long again. It is not even supper and the stars are coming out." Otto looked to the sky. With no trees blocking his view, he could see the first shimmering star peek out through the steely blue blanket. At their feet, hoofprints from Babe and the horses littered the ground, and scattered in every direction were the tracks of other animals that had come out to see what damage had been done once the men had gone to bed.

"When there's no snow, you wouldn't know half of these animals were here. People think the winter is such a dead time, but these footprints tell the real story of who lives here. I'm going to miss this place when it is time to go," said Otto.

Paul looked to the tracks at his feet. "I don't think I'll ever leave," he said. "I've spent my life carving my name into this land. Don't even know where I'd go."

Otto didn't respond, but removed his hat and dusted off the frost from the wool fibers that stuck out like guard hairs on a dog's chin. He tried to imagine the north without Paul Cunningham. He imagined drab logging camps filled with worn-down men who found no joy in their daily work. There were no songs being sung and no yarns being spun of the mythic hero Paul had become. The stories of his tall logging friend had turned the hard life of a frontier logger into something often romanticized over. Every season, young loggers showed up in camps dreaming of being the next lumberjack hero. Without Paul, the bunkhouses across the Northwoods would surely have fewer stories to tell and laughs to share. There would probably be a lot more trees left over as well. Paul sure had left his mark on the land with all the forests he helped clear.

They walked back to camp without speaking and sat down for a filling supper of stewed prunes, bacon, and pie. They hung their wet clothes near the stoves in the bunkhouse and listened to one more night of songs and laughter before the big day of work ahead of them.

––––

"Daylight in the swamp! Get on up!" the camp cook shouted the next morning into the musty bunkhouse.

After a quick, hot breakfast, Paul and Otto set off to work, slashing through the remaining trees approaching the cutline. By mid-afternoon, they had cut all but the last two. Paul had sent Babe to drag a few of the last pines down to the road while they finished the last of the claim. They trudged through the deep snow up to the last trees blazed for logging. The two men surveyed their sizes and looked back at the good work they'd done. It had been a difficult job finishing the logging in the knee-high drifts. They had earned their sleep tonight.

"This is it. The edge of our logging rights, my friend." Otto ran his hand over the logging company's mark scored into the tree.

"Well," said Paul. "What do you say? One for each of us. First tree to hit the ground decides the better jack." They were both exhausted from the morning's work, but the childlike glint in their eyes could have lit up the darkest forest.

"You have got a deal. Give the signal, and I will claim the title." Otto smiled at Paul, waiting for him to make the first move. They both stood by their trees. Paul spread his feet in the snow and held his ax to the base of the tree. He peered at Otto, who had done the same, placing the jagged teeth of his saw gently on the bark of his enormous pine. They faced each other, shirts damp from sweat and pants heavy from trudging through the tall snowdrifts. Paul's beard and Otto's mustache were filled with clumps of frost and icicles like the ones hanging from the bunkhouse roof.

Otto tightened his grip. "Ready when you are, my friend."

Paul took in a deep breath and shouted, "Go!"

They both began working with renewed enthusiasm and energy. Paul's ax swung up and down on the massive tree, dislodging large wedges of off-white, flaky pine. Otto's saw whirred back and forth, spewing sawdust with each push and pull.

"You're gonna have to catch up there, old fella!" called Paul between swings.

"I am just getting started, Bunyan!" Otto only called Paul "Bunyan" when he wanted to get under his friend's skin. It worked almost every time.

"Ha! You'd better take a break. You're looking pretty tired!"

"Not a chance," Otto called back. He paused for a split second, looking at his feet, then resumed cutting. "It might be worth taking a moment to pack down a getaway path in this snow, though."

"Oh no you don't. No excuses now. Keep cuttin' so I can beat you fair and square," Paul said.

The two kept chopping and cutting. They were getting close now, and at any moment, one of their trees would crack and start to lean. It was Otto's that gave the first sound. It was subtle, but then the snaps and cracks multiplied as the tree began to sway. Paul looked up to see his friend take the lead. He gave one more mighty swipe, and his tree began speaking as well.

"Ha ha! I think mine'll fall first," Paul called over to Otto, whose head was turned upwards, looking to the peak of his toppling giant.

It happened in an instant. A look of concern and realization flashed across Otto's face as the tree in front of him began to twist at its base. Otto glanced to his feet, which were knee-deep in heavy snow. He turned to Paul while hopping backward and, losing his balance in the process, yelled, "Get back!" As the words left his lips, the tree made a loud, final snap before pouncing back toward Otto and slamming him in the chest like a battering ram. His body shot through the air, arms and legs extended outwards as if reaching for his saw. He landed in the snow fifteen feet from where he had stood a fraction of a second before.

Paul's tree had begun to fall in the opposite direction. Paul dropped his ax and ran to his friend. He found Otto with a shocked look on his face, dark blood trickling from the sides of his mouth. Paul fell to his knees and placed one hand behind Otto's head and the other on his chest. "Otto. Otto. Hey. Look at me. Look at me!"

Otto was taking rapid, shallow breaths. His head bobbed as he turned his glossy-eyed gaze to Paul. He looked at Paul for a few seconds before splitting a weak smile beneath his large, bright-red mustache. His teeth were pink with blood. He took in a couple more shallow breaths, then said, "Beat you, my friend." His smile turned to a surprised expression as he coughed and gurgled and coughed some more. Then Paul felt the muscles in Otto's neck loosen, and the light left his friend's eyes.

Paul sat, holding Otto's head in his lap. He sat until the snow covered his shoulders like a blanket and the sky became pink with dusk. He sat until his friend felt as cold and stiff as the trees that lay fallen behind them. Paul didn't cry. He didn't shout or throw a fit of rage. He just sat with his friend in his arms and only moved when Babe finally walked back up the logging road, an empty sled dragging behind him.

The sounds of Babe's footsteps moved into Paul's consciousness, pulling him back to the last remnants of pastel in the darkening sky and sparkling blue snow around him. The ground was covered with pine needles and sawdust from Otto's blade. Paul felt warm breath at his neck. The caribou gently nuzzled his shoulder as if to say, "It's time, Paul. We've gotta go." As if to reinforce the suggestion further, a raven circling high above their heads let out three coarse caws before flying out of sight. Its silhouette looked lonely against the now gray, featureless sky.

Using his ax as a shovel, Paul dug through the heavy snow to the frozen ground beneath them. He swung the metal blade into the dirt and chipped away through roots and rock-hard soil. The light was fading fast, and he wasn't making much progress. Somewhere behind him, Babe gave a snort.

"I know, alright! We can't bury him here." Paul looked around, exasperated, his eyes landing on Otto's pale-blue face. The blood at his lips looked black in the dim light, the same way a lake looks when there is no moon.

"I just don't want some animal to come and start chewing on him before he sleeps a while." The thought of wolves and coyotes tugging at Otto's clothes gave Paul a shiver. "There was a little pond up by that creek, wasn't there?"

He picked up Otto's saw and strapped it to Babe along with his ax, then heaved Otto's heavy body over his shoulders like a large piece of lumber. They walked past the logging line and through the trees until they reached the small lake, now covered with a thick layer of snow and ice.

Paul gently laid Otto down in the snow and stepped onto the

pond. He walked to the center of the clearing where the water would be deepest and used the sides of his boots to kick away the white blanket at his feet, revealing the ice below. A hollow booming sound echoed beneath him as the ice expanded with the dropping temperature. Tiny bubbles stood suspended in the thick glass that closed off the watery nothingness. Paul went back and took the ax and saw from Babe, then returned to the naked ice.

"Stay there," Paul said to Babe. "Won't take long."

He chipped a hole in the ice with his ax until water began to gurgle through the opening. The pond around him boomed and cracked, but the ice was more than a foot thick, more than strong enough to hold Paul. He edged the saw blade into the crack and began cutting out a rectangle of ice. Once the block was free, he pushed it down and slid it under the ice shelf, leaving behind a doorway to open water lapping against the edges of the hole. He walked back to Otto, looking at the pale face. His eyes, barely open, looked like smooth, gray stones.

Everything I touch falls to the ground, thought Paul.

Paul kneeled and picked up his friend's body, then carried him to the hole in the pond, which was already covered by a delicate crystalized window of ice. He used the toe of his boot to break the glassy surface.

"G'night, friend. Rest easy." Paul clenched his teeth as his eyes glistened, and he slid his friend into the black water and beneath the snowy ice like a log being sent down the river. He turned around and walked to Babe.

"Let's get back to camp. We've got a lot of trees to skid tomorrow." Paul placed the equipment on Babe's back, and the two walked through the snowy, moonlit woods towards camp. Paul kept his hand on the back of Babe's neck the entire way, clenching a fistful of fur, assurance that his last friend wouldn't leave him anytime soon.

———

The men back in camp couldn't believe that Otto Walta was dead. He had been nearly as big of a legend as Paul. For him to die seemed like an omen that the good ole days of logging could be coming to an end. And just like with Hinckley, there was no way Paul could stay with the company after Otto's death. Once the last log was hauled to the river, he packed his things and moved right on out of camp looking for the next available job. There was no reason to be picky anymore. A tree was a tree just as much as an ax was an ax.

As Paul and Babe continued to work through the north country, a seemingly endless supply of trees was being whittled down and pushed to further reaches of the state. Not only were the old-growth, six-foot-wide pines a rarity, so were a lot of the animals and people that came with them. Walking into camp one day, one of the new sawmen looked at Babe with a shocked expression slapped across his face.

"Is that a caribou?! I didn't think any of 'em were left 'round here. Where'd you get 'em?"

"Don't matter where I found him," said Paul. "Just matters that he can haul as much timber as a team of four horses. And you won't hear him whinny or whine about it neither." *Come to think of it,* Paul thought, *I haven't seen much of Babe's kind either.* He couldn't remember the last time he had come across any sign of caribou. When he first arrived in Minnesota, it wasn't uncommon to see a herd from time to time. The cruisers talked about it often and would carry home large antler sheds like trophies to show what lurks in the wilderness. The Ojibwe relied on the caribou for their meat and hides in the past, but because they were restricted to the reservations these days, Paul suspected they hadn't seen any either. Instead, more and more deer found their way around the camps. The whitetails were a nuisance more than anything else, but at least it provided for some good venison.

But it wasn't just the animals and the scenery that were starting to look different. When it came to the logging industry, things were changing in a way that most could barely tolerate.

For most of his logging career, Paul had essentially been able to log as he pleased. It was quick and easy. The timber cruisers would find the land with the best trees, keeping the secret close to their chests, and reserve it at the land office. Then the barons would pick it up for a little over a dollar per acre. That's when the jacks and logging roads would come in and clean it up.

Years after the Hinckley fire, another blaze tore through the towns of Baudette and Spooner, causing the government to implement a new set of forestry restrictions and management plans by way of a young veteran named Christopher Andrews. He was given an official title and position to oversee the use of the woodlands, or so Paul had heard. *Probably never spent a day in his life carrying an ax*, he thought bitterly as the men around the campfire criticized the new regulations. There were new rules about how logging was to be done and how the slash was to be managed. All of it brought the pace of logging to a near standstill.

"If there was ever anything that could ruin logging, it would be a politician." The jacks nodded in agreement to Paul's comment. A few even raised their teacups.

Sure, there were fires from time to time from the countless piles of slash scattered throughout the territory lighting up during heat waves or left along railroads and catching sparks cast off the tracks, but the loggers, like most people, didn't want to be told what to do. Still, money moves the world, and if they didn't follow the new regulations, they wouldn't get paid.

When Paul tried to remember his logging days after the fire, there were years of dense fog clouding his memories. He really couldn't discern one year from the next. Only a few events stood out in his mind. The day he lost Otto and the day the new logging regulations were announced were a couple of examples. Another was when he lifted a large pile of logs off a group of men that were trapped beneath, setting off another swarm of fairytales, or when he and Babe cleared more board feet of wood in a day than any man had before in logging history.

Then there was the late summer morning, a little over thirteen years after Otto had died and close to fifteen since losing Amelia, when that awful rabbit hopped back into camp. Paul had just stepped out of the bunkhouse and was on his way to the stable when he saw it. The hair on his arms stood straight up as he watched the animal move over to Babe and use its small button nose to nudge him awake. As Babe stirred, the cottontail darted away, leaving Paul to fear the unknown damage that could be coming. *Every time I see you,* he thought, *you bring destruction. What's next? What do you want? What else do I have to lose?*

With this last thought, his eyes turned to Babe, who woke up and lifted his head to look around camp. Babe stretched, gave a sleepy yawn, and stood up, looking at Paul. He started to walk in Paul's direction, but staggered with an odd lean to the right the same way Ola Värmlänning walked after a long night in the saloon. Babe's head was tilted at an awkward angle, and he kept shaking it as if to clear a haze from his vision. Paul's friend was well past the age of any normal caribou, and his size was exceptional to be sure, more like a large bull moose than anything. He rarely showed any sign of age or fatigue, just like Paul. This new behavior was not only odd but exactly what Paul had feared when he saw that rabbit wake up Babe.

"No. You can't take Babe," he said, thinking of the hare that was now long gone. Paul didn't know how, but he knew it was the same creature that he had seen all through his logging life. It didn't seem possible, but there was no mistaking the look on that rabbit's face. He recognized it the same way he could tell his teacup from all the others in camp even though they all looked the same. The same way he knew his dreams of Amelia were more than just dreams. This rabbit was real, and it was the same one he had seen time and time again, the same awful beast that had haunted him for years.

When Paul spoke, Babe looked up at him with wide eyes like he'd been doused with cold water. He stomped his front right hoof into the dirt, shivered, straightened up, then walked toward Paul as if the episode had never happened.

"You alright there?" Paul scratched Babe behind the ears, who snorted happily in response.

But the episodes of stumbling and poor coordination went on for several weeks, coming in increasing waves of intensity. One day, Babe would be just fine, hauling massive loads of wood down the skid roads, but the next, he could barely stand. After a half day of work, his knobby knees would shake like trembling leaves and he would collapse to the ground. When Babe finally made it to his feet, he'd swerve back and forth until he found Paul's chest. His pleading eyes stared at Paul with a frightened expression that made Paul feel sick to his stomach. In those moments, Paul would end up lifting Babe over his shoulders, carrying him back to camp to rest.

"What's up with Babe, Paul?" one of the shanty men asked one evening after dinner.

"Ah, nothin'. He's just got a little bug or something. That's all," Paul replied. "He'll be back to himself in no time, I reckon."

Outwardly, Paul kept a smile on for Babe. Inside, he was pleading for his friend to start moving in the right direction, but as the weeks went by, there were more and more days where Babe was unable to walk, even days where he didn't seem to recognize his only friend.

It was a cold, rainy day in late September when Paul walked into the stables and found Babe lying in the corner of the dark, musty shack. The other horses were huddled at the far end of the pens, stamping their feet nervously. Paul walked slowly through the dark and knelt down next to him. He ran his hand down the long, smooth antlers and rubbed Babe behind the ears. The caribou's eyelids twitched, and he puffed a short breath out his nostrils.

"Hey there, Babe. You're gonna be just fine, ya hear me?" Paul said.

The skin around Babe's eyes creased with a grimace as he tilted his head and gazed at Paul with empty eyes. If there was any recognition in those eyes, it only lasted a fraction of a second before it slipped away. Paul was lost to him. Babe looked more like a wild animal than ever before, helpless and scared as the day they had found each other. His massive antlers finally turned to the side and rested on the mossy earth. His eyes closed, and he exhaled a breath that never seemed to end. When it did, there was no inhale to follow.

Paul sat in the darkness, feeling empty and alone. He kept his hand on Babe's head and wished he could melt away into the black surrounding them. The boards of the shed rattled as a wet gust blew through the forest, clearing trees of their leaves for the season. The mist settled on Paul's bare cheeks, and he shivered.

"Babe, I'm gonna...it's gonna be fine, okay?" Paul drove his hands under the belly of his friend and lifted him up. The body was still warm, but the heat would soon be gone. Once outside the stable, he heaved Babe over his head and carried him across his shoulders the same way an ox holds a yolk. Not a word was spoken as the shanty men watched the titanic sight, Paul Bunyan carrying his massive companion across his back, out of camp, and into the logged lands. He carried Babe to a nearby lake and set him down facing the setting sun, which was trying fruitlessly to peek through the rain clouds that hung like veils from the sky. Paul slid the harness over Babe's ears and nose and walked away from his friend, never looking back.

After that, there were no more smiles around the campfire. No more joining in with the camp songs. No more joy from the final crunch of a falling tree landing on the forest floor. After Babe's death, Paul lost something in his stature. Whether he actually was shorter, or he just didn't feel like fighting gravity, no one knows, but he didn't carry himself the way he once did. It was as if his once monstrous frame was beaten down and tarnished, like the head of an ax that had taken too many hits from the blacksmith's hammer.

He moved from camp to camp for several years, finally settling in Virginia, Minnesota, with the Rainy Lake Lumber Company. They had been the biggest mill in the world, so they say, building close to one hundred and fifty camps with almost five thousand men employed during the busiest seasons. But, just like the four-hundred-year-old white pines, all giants eventually fall, and after five years of bringing in an innumerable amount of pines, poplars, cedars, and birches for the company, Paul could see that the end of his logging days was near. The old trees were virtually all gone, and folks were struggling to reestablish them. Deer were coming in and eating the saplings, and the trees brought over from Europe to jumpstart the population were catching blister rust. This, in turn, was beginning to attack the native white pines. For Paul, it felt like it was all coming to an end, and sure enough, in 1929, Rainy Lake Lumber Company closed its doors for good, leaving him out in the cold, wandering the wasteland he had helped create.

Inside the mill, Paul strapped Otto's old saw to his back along with Babe's old harness. He grabbed his oiled ax handle and swung it over his shoulder. A rucksack filled with a few possessions dangled loosely from the double-bit ax. Pausing at the doorway, he looked back into the eerily still building. Saws stood motionless, and all the piles of lumber once stacked to the ceiling were gone. Paul slumped his shoulders, losing an inch in height, and walked out of the sawdust into the fresh air, aspen seeds floating by in a gust of wind. He followed the haphazard path of cotton-like seeds as they danced into the sky away from the town of Virginia, Minnesota, where carriages pulled by horses and an occasional motorcar roamed like ants scurrying this way and that, creating a dizzying commotion that made Paul feel sick. He dropped his head and began walking away from the town and the noise.

"Say, Tryg, is that who I think it is?" a voice called from behind Paul. He didn't turn around, but recognized the voice as one of the two bouncing Norwegians who had once traveled miles upon miles just to work alongside the logging legend.

"Who?" a second man responded.

"There, just up there, walking away. Doesn't that look like Paul Bunyan?"

"Him? No. He's not tall enough. And Nils, I hate to say it, but I think I heard Paul Bunyan died, or he walked north or maybe west with his big deer or something. Can't remember for sure, but that's not him."

"You sure? I could have sworn it looked like him," Nils said.

"You're just hungry," said Tryg. "Come on. If we dawdle any longer, we'll miss our train."

Paul couldn't blame the Norwegian for not recognizing him. As far as he was concerned, there wasn't much to look at anymore.

After leaving the area, Paul followed a chain of rivers and lakes that led northeast past several towns. He slept on the east side of the lakes each night to wake with the sun, and if it wasn't for the warm light, he was sure he'd never wake up. In a word, he was aimless. An arrow without a target. An ax without a tree. He didn't have a plan. He just followed his feet, and his feet followed the water. Soon, Paul saw fewer and fewer people. He knew Ely was somewhere to the west and considered swinging over to pick up supplies, but instead continued northeast until he came to a moderately-sized lake with water clear and cold. He skipped over a stream flowing south from the lakeshore and rested on a small peninsula. The signs of logging were all around him. Trees had been cleared, leaving behind slash and debris, but all the people were gone and the shrubs and blueberry bushes were starting to fill in. Paul explored a nearby ghost camp where he found some cookware, old sheets, and blankets in a half-collapsed shanty.

He spent the next week sorting the forgotten lumber and logs, nails, and assorted tools. With the addition of a few more small trees cut down, he finished the job of repurposing all the wood into a single-room, wood-floor cabin with a simple porch. When it was complete, he sat outside, his back resting against a large stump, and contemplated the little shack.

Home, Paul thought with a tired sigh.

Otto's saw, tarnished and dull, leaned against the wall by the door and sagged under its own weight. Babe's harness hung from a nail. Reminders of friendship. Reminders of loss.

Turning his gaze from the relics, he stared at the blank walls. "A window and a chair would be nice. Maybe a bed? We'll make it work." Paul's lone voice cutting through the forest silence accentuated his solitude.

He figured he could head back to Ely, eventually, to find some windowpanes, maybe a water basin of some sort. The chair and the bed he could make. That was all he needed. But for now, all of that seemed like too much work. Paul walked into the empty cabin, lay down on his back on the wooden floorboards, and stared at the ceiling. Light peered in through cracks all around him. He didn't move for hours but watched as the shadows stretched their way across the walls, and bit by bit, the cabin became dark like the life he had grown into. Paul closed his eyes and imagined that the wooden box he lay in was a coffin and the little drops of rain now tapping on the roof was the dirt covering him up for good.

He thought of all the trees he had felled. Millions of acres of ancient forests, gone. His parents, gone. Otto and Babe, gone. Amelia, gone. And yet, here he remained, sitting alone in a landscape as scarred as he was. Paul looked at his hands, beaten by labor and time. He thought of the conversation he had with Otto a long time ago on a lonely night on the shores of a small lake, with Babe resting nearby, when he asked Otto if the pain of loss would ever fade.

"No, I don't think so," Otto had said to Paul. "Not completely, anyway. I've got scars on my arms that don't hurt like the cuts that caused them, but the memories are still there. Like these lights. They'll burn out tonight, but we'll still see them when we close our eyes."

Now, sitting alone, Paul spoke to his long-gone friend and the ceiling above him. "I think you're right, Otto. But I think the hurtin' is the same as the scars, and I don't think it ever goes away."

The walls of the cabin and the woods around him didn't respond, so Paul shut his eyes tight and tried to fall asleep.

The Man in the Woods

Find me in the darkness
Waiting there for thee
When your ears are ready to listen
And your eyes ready to see
Find me in the darkness
Standing in the trees

Time is a funny thing. Just like scooping handfuls of water from a clear lake, there is no doubt that you hold it in your hands. You see your reflection in it. You feel the weight, and your hands are cold and wet. But just as certain as you can grab it, it slips through the folds of your skin. The tighter you pinch your fingers together, the more it escapes you. Time escapes in the same way. When you are drifting aimlessly, it soars past you as silent and unknowing as the flight of an owl on a moonless night. Paul did add the stone sink and a few windows to the cabin, but dust had gathered and the glass had withered like freshly picked flowers left in the sunlight. And slowly but surely, Paul Cunningham grew older. His skin began to wrinkle, and gray hairs started to find their way to his chin and temples the same way a lake begins freezing over in the winter. The weight of his sadness shrunk him closer to the size of mortal men.

Mostly, Paul walked through the woods without purpose. Time's passage was only marked by the changing seasons and the thickness of the blankets of moss covering the wooden roof. Warm, lush summers faded to falling leaves, which landed into accumulating snow that eventually melted, giving way to frustratingly eager, brilliantly green spring.

In the summers, he missed his parents. He would think of his father working in the yard and his mother calling him in to wash up before dinner. In the winters, it was Amelia's soft, warm skin he missed most. He couldn't think of a greater contrast to the harsh cold than her gentle touch.

Paul saw her in the lone loon, calling out across the glassy water in the last light of the day. She was the first maple tree blazing bright before all others even thought of changing colors. She was the burnt moon hanging low over the lake in late autumn. In all the ways Paul saw Amelia, it was never long enough, and the aching emptiness remained.

But on one humid summer night, the cycle broke. In his sleep, Paul found himself facing his mother's loving, open arms. It was his first dream since Babe died many years before.

"Mama?" Paul's sadness and joy merged into a feeling of relief. In an instant, the weight of his solitude lifted. He had been lost at sea for more years than he could count, and finally, he had the first sight of dry land.

"Hello, Paul." Her smile was familiar and comforting. She was the strong mother of his childhood. He looked to his hands, which were slender and callous-free. A boy of carefree whimsy and innocence was summed up in his shaggy locks of dark hair. He ran to her.

"I've missed ya, Mama." He held her tightly, feeling safe and secure blanketed by her embrace.

"I know." She ran a hand gently through his hair. "You've been working hard. Just look at how the land has changed." She gestured at the forest around them. They were in Maine and Michigan. Wisconsin and Minnesota. Slash and tree stumps covered the land. Small streams of smoke snaked up from the ground here and there. Logs jammed up the rivers. They could see for hundreds of miles. A herd of white-tailed deer, startled by the spectators, scattered before them.

Paul tried to take in the magnitude of the scarred land surrounding him. "Did I do this?" He took a step back from his mother. "It can't be this bad."

"It doesn't look very good, does it?" Samantha said.

"I don't even remember how it looked before." He squinted and tried to imagine an untouched, old-pine forest but gave in to the desolate scenery in front of him.

Samantha looked at her son and smiled. "It looked like this." The ground shook as a world of pines shot into the air, surrounding them. In a flash, Paul and Samantha were floating high above the endless sea of dark, emerald-green pines that were still swaying back and forth from their sudden arrival. The only breaks in the trees below them were the scattered lakes and streams sparkling in the sunlight. Paul wasn't sure, but he thought he could see herds of caribou running up streambeds and Native Americans gathering at the shore of one of the lakes.

Paul was stunned into silence.

"It really is amazing, isn't it?" his mother said. "You know, Paul, you can't bring us back, but you can make us proud."

"What do ya mean? Make who proud?" asked Paul.

"All of us. Me. Your father. Otto and Amelia." She laughed. "Babe. You have a gift. You've done more than anyone to shape this land, but it came with a price. Now it's time to bring the pines back. It is time for you to protect this place."

"So, you want me to plant trees?" Paul was confused. He tried to think of how his logging could have led to the losses he and those around him suffered, but he couldn't think clearly. This disorienting dream caused his mind to feel thick and slow.

All of a sudden, Paul felt his body lengthening and watched his hands become that of the man he had been. As he grew, his mother shrank. At first, Paul thought it was an illusion, but as he kept watching, he realized that she was getting smaller still. Her head bowed down, and she sank into a pile of linen clothes. In the blouse was a small, moving mass.

The story of how he came to his parents' doorstep all those years ago in a winter storm came to his mind, but out of the folds, instead of a child, the familiar soft rabbit emerged. It crawled out and looked up at Paul. Then, it opened its mouth and spoke with the voice of his mother. "Paul, it is time for you to go. You must wake. You must begin your work."

The rabbit continued, this time not with his mother's voice, but with a deeper, male voice that contained a subtle accent. "I've watched you for a long time. You are finally ready to begin the good work." As it spoke, it began to change again. This time, the rabbit was turning back into a human. The gray fur with the rusty patch was traded for tanned skin and shining black hair, dark as volcanic glass. The man wore pants made of animal hides, and his chest was bare save for his braided hair draping over his shoulder. The sweet, earthy smell of cedar filled the air around him.

Paul thought he would be angry to see the rabbit in the dream, but he wasn't. The rabbit had been at his side during some of the worst times in his life, and Paul had always assumed that it was the cause of his torment and torture. But in this place, he wasn't so sure.

Paul had lived a life larger and longer than it should have been, and he felt stretched thin. His mind spun with all he had seen. Knowing he lacked the energy to witness much else in this dream, Paul surrendered with a sigh and a question. "Who are you?" he asked.

"I am Nanabush," said the dark-haired man. "I have lived on this land longer than the trees that you logged. I have watched fires burn and floods rage. I have seen the disease that steals the minds of the deer. And I have seen the lands heal when the time is right. It is time for them to heal again. It is your job to help the healing begin."

Paul shook his head, trying to piece everything together. "Are you... is this real, or am I dreaming?"

"It is both. Tomorrow, this dream will be a memory. Are the memories of the ones you have loved any different than what you have seen today? Remember what you have seen here. Remember what you have heard, and it will be real. But for now, Paul Cunningham, you must remember what Amelia Brennen told you. And you must wake. Wake!" The man reached out and shook Paul by the shoulders.

Paul bolted upright and opened his eyes to silver moonlight streaming through the window in his small cabin, words of the dream echoing in his head. His hemlock-woven cot creaked beneath him as he swung his feet over the edge of the bed, images of his mother, the rabbit, and the tanned man spinning in his mind, losing form with every breath. He squeezed his eyes shut to hold onto the images and solidify each word. He thought of the trees he had cut. Those mammoth, strong trees had lived for hundreds of years. He thought of Amelia, Babe, and Otto, and all the others who died in the fires as bystanders in his pursuit of greatness. Amelia had pressed him once on the logging. She seemed to see the danger in the line he was walking, but Paul never could quite understand what she was really saying.

Then, as if a lantern had turned on in the dark cabin, he saw his journey from a new vantage point. Paul had moved across hundreds of miles, tearing down pillars that had served as a home to people and animals long before him. He had been part of a wave pushing westward, displacing everything and anyone who didn't belong. It made him sick as he thought back on his life and what he considered his triumphant and nearly heroic abilities. Now, he saw them as devastation and, even worse, a part in the loss of the only thing that he had ever adored more than logging. Amelia.

Paul hunched over with his hands on his thighs, dry-heaving as bile burned its way through his throat. Wiping his mouth with his sleeve, he lay back in bed, and, trying to drive the faces of Amelia and his mother from his mind, he turned his thoughts to Babe. But he didn't see the memory of the healthy, playful animal. Instead, it was the weary, confused, stumbling beast stricken with a disease likely caught from the deer who had moved north because of Paul's sharp ax. He rolled onto his side and convulsed, tears streaming down his face.

Outside the cabin, a small rabbit lay down on the wooden planks of the porch, waiting for the aging man inside to fall asleep again, hoping he would wake ready to find a way to help the forest heal. He would need to seek help, for one thing was certain. He wouldn't be able to do it alone.

———

The next day, Paul woke to July sunshine raining through the slats in the cabin walls. His head felt as if it had been split in two by his ax, but for the first time in a long while, he felt energized. He closed his eyes and could still see his mother, who turned into the rabbit, which turned into the tan-skinned man. Their words were clear, and he knew he needed to rebuild the Northwoods. Unfortunately, not only was Paul struggling to think of something Amelia would have said to help him with his new purpose, but he had no idea how to start the mission that was set upon him.

Should he cut down the competing trees or plant new ones? Where should he start working? He walked for days looking for something that would show him how to begin. He walked around lakes and up hills, but all he saw were the same scenes of old logging roads, dilapidated camps, thick underbrush, and piles of slash. In the years since logging had died out, plenty of small hardwoods and aspens had cropped up. Scattered pines grew here and there, stunted by their competition. And he couldn't walk more than two hundred yards without running into grazing deer. It seemed the wolves and few mountain lions that remained couldn't keep up with the number of deer now roaming the northern lands.

Sick of his own indecisiveness, Paul decided to start clearing the groves of aspen and hardwood saplings. As long as those were there, the deer could come in and feed. Also, if he wanted the pines to return, he needed to either find seedlings to transplant or make some with gathered pine cones. The largest trees were always the best producers of cones, but no one had thought about replacing the trees harvested until far too late in the game, so his best options were to find scattered seedlings that had woken from their dormancy or locate the white pines that were too small to harvest but were now starting to produce offspring. He could collect the seedlings and, one by one, transplant them into new groves. Just to be sure they would be safe, he would use old fallen trees, young aspens, and scattered slash for fencings around the acreages. The last thing he wanted was to find deer tearing up his young pines.

He was actually quite proud of himself for coming up with the plan. Since the weather would be good for a couple more months, Paul decided to start as far from the cabin as possible. Sure, it would take a long time, and he wasn't as fast as he used to be, but he figured that since he caused most of this mess, it might as well be him who fixes it, one tree at a time.

———

In the early years after meeting Nanabush in the dream, Paul walked far and wide to start his work. That first summer, he walked as far as he could, ax and saw strapped across his back, chewing on pine needles like toothpicks. He walked until the lakes became so clustered together that he knew the logging camps wouldn't have traveled much farther north. He then turned south and targeted every logging road, aspen grove, and old clearing, all signs of the abandoned industry.

The sun was high when he set his ax and saw down to walk the first large patch of leafy trees all reaching well above his head. It was amazing how such slender and flimsy trees could squelch the world beneath their leaves of any real sunshine. And hidden beneath these taller trees were plenty of small white pines scraping the bottom of his kneecaps. They all seemed to be waiting like children in a hungry crowd, hoping for a chance at getting their hands on handouts of food or spare change but too short to compete with the unknowing and, likely, uncaring adults. Maybe that was all they needed. Just a chance to compete. Just a little sunshine.

Paul reached down to the base of the nearest aspen, the peppered bark smooth to the touch and soothing on his beaten hands. The trunk was three to four inches wide. Paul wrapped his fingers around the base and squatted down. He took a deep breath, then heaved his body upwards. He strained against the tree's roots, which were holding on for dear life, unwilling to lose this battle of tug-of-war. He thought he could feel all of the neighboring aspens clinging their fine network of roots into that of their neighbor who was under this sudden attack.

For a moment, Paul thought the tree might not budge, but then a small pop reverberated in his palms. He pursed his lips and blew a thin stream of air outwards. Another pop gave way to a succession of snaps, like a breaking dam, and the tree began to give. He stood up with a loud yell, holding the tree and its soil-filled roots high above his head.

A wave of exhaustion crashed down on him, and he broke out in an itchy, uncomfortable sweat.

"Well, that's one way to do it," he said.

Paul could have sworn that he saw the small pine by his feet lean into the new window of sunlight, eager for a view of the world above. He looked around to the hundreds of other trees all similar in size. The thought of pulling all of them out made his fatigue intensify.

"Maybe a few years ago I could'a pulled 'em all. Gonna have to come up with somethin' else."

Paul looked to his ax instead. He choked up on the handle like it was a hatchet and grabbed another nearby aspen. Bending the tree, he struck it with the ax, slicing straight through the sapling about six inches off the ground.

"Now that wasn't so bad," he said, smiling.

And that's how he continued. If the saplings were extremely thin, Paul would pull them out, but anything bigger than a couple inches across was neatly pruned at its base by his ax and tossed to the nearest fence line, sometimes up to fifty feet away. It seemed that this newest project had given him some of his youthful strength back. The pines, finally uncovered, would shoot up to the newly discovered sunlight, realizing their potential. It was as if they were simply biding their time, waiting for the chance to seize a ray of sunshine and climb it.

From the start, Paul built crosshatched fences using the aspens and stray fallen Norwegian and jack pines to keep the deer away from his young crop. He admitted that this was likely a losing battle, but to him, the deer were a bitter reminder of the changes he had brought upon the land, so it was worth the effort.

For the areas cleared without any established small pine trees, Paul would circle the spot with an old sheet slung over his shoulder, using the folds of the fabric to cradle all the pine cones and saplings he could scavenge. He'd return to the clearing and spread the young pines and cones over the land like Johnny Appleseed.

In the winter, and in the spring before the ground would thaw, he would focus on thinning out the underbrush that surrounded the young pines and rebuilding fences around the groves.

No longer looking to prove his ability to withstand the harshest elements, Paul chose to keep close to the cabin when big winter storms moved through. After the storms passed, he took the opportunity to survey the groves and the fence lines, looking for fresh tracks in the snow that might share the secrets of the thieving beasts who aimed to threaten his work. On one such trip, Paul followed the pawprints of a playful marten. It must have been enjoying itself in the fresh snow, for the footprints went on for nearly a mile. When the marten's tracks disappeared into a large snowbank, Paul looked towards the nearby fence line of a pine grove he had finished planting the previous autumn. There, gathered around a small part in the crosshatched fence, he noticed a group of hoofprints and clusters of droppings.

"Oh no you don't. You're not getting in there if I have anything to say about it." Paul readjusted the fence and tightened the weave of branches, peering to the other side to be sure that there was no sign of invasion. Then he gave the barrier a few good shakes. Satisfied, he turned towards home, hoping to see signs of the marten one more time.

As the years passed, Paul found it harder and harder to spend extended hours in the cold, and whether he would admit it or not, he couldn't cover the ground he used to. His only company came from the small rabbit with its twitchy whiskers and rusty hair behind its neck. It never spoke to him as it had in the dream, but Paul found himself starting to talk to it from time to time as if it could understand his words.

Paul would go for weeks on end without seeing the furry face, but just when he began to forget that the animal was a part of his story, there it was. It would follow him on his longer trips to the farthest fields, darting across some of the young groves. When he came close enough, Paul would often extend a question, hoping he might hear a response.

"Now where've you been these last few days?" Paul would ask.

But all he got was a wiggle of the nose and a shake of the whiskers, at best a quick blink, and the rabbit would dart off again. Paul didn't know for sure who or what the rabbit was, but from the dreams and from everywhere it had been in his life, he kept hoping that one day it would answer him.

It went on like this until one day, sitting on the edge of his bed in the soft morning sunlight, Paul ran his hands through his hair and brought them down to his knees. In between his fingers were four silver strands.

I sure am gettin' old, aren't I? he thought.

The hairs were coarse, and they curled around his fingers, reflecting the golden rays of dawn's light coming through the window.

I don't feel that old. But even as he thought it, a familiar ache spread through his knuckles. *Mmmm...who am I kiddin'?* His hands and knees had become a reliable tell for rapid changes in humidity and the storms that followed. His clothes had gotten baggier over the years, and he didn't have to duck through the doorframe anymore.

"Well, just a few more seasons. Maybe then I can rest."

The Beginning, Summer 1983

Cracking and popping,
Branches snap
When a tall tree begins swinging down,
Tearing through the forest,
Descending to the floor.
She inhales suddenly, gasping,
and the tree hits the ground.
The silence that follows is broken by a breeze
Which bows the heads of the neighboring trees,
Acknowledging their fallen friend.

Paul Cunningham woke the morning after the dream bitter and restless.

So it begins. So it ends, he thought. *I came into this world alone. Might as well leave it that way.*

It had been a long time since he had dreamed of Amelia. The image of her soft vanilla blouse, deep chestnut dress, and slanted smile was as clear as if she were standing in front of him now. The thought of her calling out to him, engulfed in flames, was a painful surprise he had hoped he would never see again.

What did she mean by "help"? Does it even matter anymore?

Paul swung his legs over the bed and felt the aches of the previous day's work. It was his last grove. He had finished the work he set out to do. The thought of the miles traveled and acres planted made him want to lie back down and sleep forever. He knew that some of his trees likely didn't take, but he would continue to walk the miles and keep an eye on things as best he could until he finally passed into the next world.

What else is there to do? What else can I do?

From time to time, he'd seen folks hiking or camping in the distance and thought about sharing his story.

What good would that do? They don't need to know my business.

The truth was, Paul wasn't even sure what year it was. Could have been 1950, could have been the 1960s. He'd lost track long ago after he realized that the reforestation he'd begun didn't really bring Amelia back. He was no closer to her, Babe, Otto, or his parents than he'd been when he started this all. Unless you count the fact that he was a crooked old man and could die at any moment. In that way, he was maybe as close as one could get to a reunion with the dead.

As for the work he had done over the years, he had to admit that he was finally feeling good about something again. The last time he had felt this proud was when Babe was alive and they were logging unlike anyone ever known. Now, he had successfully replanted more trees than anyone in the world as far as he knew. *Save maybe God, I suppose.* Every time he walked through the Northwoods and saw his trees growing, he smiled.

Paul decided that he needed to take one more look at yesterday's finished product, so he slowly got dressed, grabbed his old ax, and headed out the door. He first went to the lake to wash his face and clean off his spare pair of pants. After noticing that his ax had a few small specks of rust along the blades, he took a half hour to sharpen it before heading out to the grove. It was about noon before he reached the bramble of wood he'd built as a fence around his freshly planted trees. He stopped at the edge, getting ready to slowly scale the fence, when he heard the noise.

Paul fixed his eyes on the ground, straining to pull the sound in closer to his eardrums. It was a faint, rhythmic noise of soft grinding and tearing with occasional pops and cracks. He had only listened for a fraction of a second when it occurred to him what it was. Paul's skin went ash white as he looked up to see a small herd of deer, maybe twenty in total, breaking off young branches and chewing the soft, long, blue-green needles of the infant pines that had been recently planted. To his far right, he saw an area of broken-down fencing, the trespassers' likely entrance.

A volcanic fury began to boil up inside of him. It started as a spark in his belly and quickly filled him with the same flames that had once destroyed his future.

"Hey! HEY! Get out of here! ARGH!" The sour hatred racing through his bones was blinding and white hot. He hurled his ax in the direction of the already disappearing, bouncing whitetails, who had squeezed through another small hole in the nearby fence. The ax barely made it over the fence. Paul lost his balance climbing through the bramble of dead aspens and fell to his knees, adding to the pains of his degenerating joints. He tried to get up, but with one leg caught on a branch, he fell onto his face, making a soft thud like an old, rotten log landing on a bed of moss.

"Get off me!" Paul said as he struggled with his tangled leg. "Let me go!" He fought with the branches that were grabbing onto him like starving hands outside a soup kitchen until he finally broke free and climbed to his feet, panting and spitting like an old, rabid dog. He looked up to the damage in front of him, and his spirit shattered. The deer had demolished the grove. Pines everywhere were stripped clean of their young needles or, even worse, snapped and left hanging at odd angles. Paul felt violated. He crumbled to the ground in a limp heap and sobbed. His entire life had been spent working towards what he thought was right, and it continued to end in loss and pain. He logged the trees and lost his love. He planted the trees and lost his spirit and strength.

Paul leaned back against the pile of wood, resting his head and looking up at the open sky. "How am I supposed to do this?" he said to the clouds. His mind was racing, looking for anything to cling to. "I clear and clean up the land. I plant thousands of trees and protect them. And what is it for? I CAN'T DO THIS ANYMORE!" Paul slammed his fists into the ground repeatedly.

He had reached the climax of his anger and sadness and began to tumble into his defeat. He closed his eyes and spoke to himself. "Oh, Paul. Paul, Paul, Paul..."

Seeking comfort, he reached a hand into the neck of his shirt and ran his fingers down a metal chain, clenching his fist on a tarnished, misshapen locket. He slowed his breathing and smelled the fresh pine resin heating up in the sun. He rocked back and forth, eyes hidden beneath wrinkled skin, and continued trying to calm himself down.

"Oh, Paul, Paul, Paul..." he said. As his heart slowed, so did the pace and volume of his words. "Paul..." he whispered. "Paul..." He sat silently, listening to the sounds of his own breathing.

"Paul." This time, the voice wasn't his. It came from somewhere else. He held completely still, wondering if he'd imagined it but hoping for the voice to speak again.

"Paul..." the voice repeated. It was a voice he hadn't truly heard in a lifetime but knew it like his own. His heart began pumping erratically, and his body felt like it was being beckoned home.

"Paul..." Amelia's voice was calling to him from far away. He opened his eyes and reached out for her in the thick, dark, odorless smoke that surrounded him.

"Amelia?! Where are you? AMELIA!" he shouted for her, standing up and swinging his arms blindly, hoping to land on something.

"Paul...help...get help..." said Amelia.

He didn't hear fear in her voice. She had spoken these words to him before, but this time, Paul knew what she meant. He felt something rub against his bare ankle and looked down to see the rabbit. It turned its head to look at him, then puffed up its chest and opened its mouth. A cool breeze flowed from between the hare's jaws, and the smoke began to clear. And there, standing by a lone pine tree in a world of only white, stood Amelia Brennen facing Paul Cunningham. Her long-sleeved, vanilla blouse wrapped around her torso, and the chestnut folds of her dress blowing in the wind made her look like she was flying through the air.

"Amelia," Paul said. His throat was tight and he could barely breathe, but somehow he found his voice. "I've missed you so much."

"I know." She smiled. "You've been doing good work, Paul."

"I've been trying. I didn't realize...I never would have believed the cost of all this. The land. The people...the animals...you..."

They stared at each other for a long time. Paul didn't dare move. He didn't dare think. He didn't want to disturb the still waters of this dream in fear that it would vanish.

Amelia's smile disappeared. "You need help, Paul. It's time to get help. Help is the one thing you've never been able to accept, but now you have to. You can't protect the forests alone."

Paul found himself falling into her knowing eyes. He knew Amelia was right. He'd been planting and nursing trees for decades now, but what was to stop it all from going away when he was gone, or even when he was here for that matter. Just as it takes more than one person to clear a forest, it takes more than one to protect it. As if to hammer home the point, pain shot through both his knees and his back. These were pains he knew all too well from years spent working in these woods. Paul winced. Amelia's caring gaze made him long to hold her.

"I need your help, Amelia. I need you." He tried to move closer, but his feet wouldn't budge.

"You have my help. You have me." She stepped closer, standing inches from his face. "But it's time for you to find others. It's time for you to share your story. People don't know Paul Cunningham the way I do. Your memory is a lie. Paul Bunyan is a sideshow, a circus act. It's time to change that." She bent over, picked up the rabbit that was still at his feet, and scratched behinds its ears.

"It's time to go, Paul. It's time for you to wake again." Amelia stood so close that Paul could feel her breath and smell the wild mint and lilacs in her hair.

"I don't want to. I want to stay with you," he pleaded. "I don't want to be alone."

"You're not alone." She kissed him on his dry lips. Her mouth was warm and real. Amelia pulled away and stared into Paul's eyes. "And you'll be with me someday. But now, you must go. Nanabush will show you the way from here." She bent over and put the rabbit back down onto its padded feet. She took a few steps backward, facing Paul, smiling her knowing smile, then turned to walk back into the smoky void, never looking back.

Paul saw light through the darkness of his heavy, hooded eyelids. He opened his eyes to find the tattered pine grove in front of him. On the ground at his feet was the small rabbit. The animal tilted its head and looked up at him.

Paul pushed himself up to a sitting position and took a long, deep breath. "Okay...okay...I'm ready to get help. Show me what I need to do."

"Follow me," the rabbit seemed to say as it snuck through the broken fencing and began hopping south.

Paul looked back one last time at the grove and the broken saplings. He turned and saw his old, heavy ax lying at the base of the fence where it had fallen. As he reached down for it, Paul noticed smooth skin on the back of his hand. The brown spots and white hairs that had appeared on his arms and hands over the years had disappeared. He lifted the ax and was surprised by how light it felt. A wave of strength ran through his bones, and Paul straightened himself up towards the sky. He turned to look at the rabbit, which was waiting for him beyond the boundary, watching what his next move would be.

Paul put one hand on the fence and leapt over it, agile as a lynx. He brushed back the dark hair that had fallen into his eyes. As he walked toward the rabbit, the years shed, and he grew as tall as he had ever been. There was a lot of work to be done, and he would need help doing it.

The man in the pines had finally returned to the work he was always meant to do.

Epilogue

For every story, every folktale, legend, or myth, there must be a beginning. Someone must step forward and be the first one to share the journey with others. As time passes, we tend to let the cement dry on these stories. But what if we woke them back up? What if these heroes came back to life? If Paul Bunyan was a real person, how would he feel about his current image? I think if he were to walk out of the trees today, he might have a different story to tell than the one we know. I'd like to think he would become one more voice for the environment. I'd like to think that somewhere up in the Northwoods, there is one more legend taking a stand, doing his part, and asking us to be stewards of our resources in protecting this special land that we call home.

About the Author

David Nash is a Minnesota native who made his first visit to the giant, talking Paul Bunyan in Brainerd, Minnesota, before the age of six. He is an award-winning singer-songwriter, and you can find his first studio recorded album that serves as a companion to the book (also titled *The Man in the Pines*) anywhere music is streamed. He lives in Wisconsin with his wife and two children, where he works as a pediatric ophthalmologist.

www.ingramcontent.com/pod-product-compliance
Lightning Source LLC
Chambersburg PA
CBHW051300250626
47155CB00009B/3372